The Carhayaken Ring
PROJECT
Perpetuity of Humans

CARHAYAKEN RING
OUR LAST CHANCE - ONE EARTH - BILLIONS OF HUMANS

CONTENTS

Tachyon Node International Edition Issue 1

ISBN-13: 978-1-943958-01-6   ISSN 2472-5226

Universe Bound

J Carrell Jones
Publisher and Editor-in-Chief

Contributing Writers
William Hayashi
Kelly King
Patricia I. Williams
Moshe Prigan
Brandon Hill
Tachyon Node Staff
NASA

Cover Art by J Carrell Jones

Article/Story Submissions:
Publisher@universebound.space

Advertisement:
Ads@universebound.space

General Information:
Info@universebound.space or
send snail mail to:

Mythical Legends Publishing, LLC
c/o General Information
P.O. Box 1667, Inglewood, Ca. 90308

Dimensional Nexus

ROGUE'S GALLERY

Björn Malmberg
J Carrell Jones

Library of Congress Control Number: 2016907904

Printed in the United States of America
http://mythicallegends.com

EXTRASOLAR NOHAI LEGACY

In His Own Words

By William Hayashi

"Prepare to engage inter-dimensional engine," Captain Iona Babbage announced.

"Standing by on I/D Drive power up, Captain," Chief Engineer Arnold replied.

"Engage!"

The subdued low frequency hum rose in pitch as the atomic engines increased their power output into the I/D Drive, creating a bubble of the local universe around the spacecraft prior to the engines forcing the ship from our universe into the space in between the infinite universes in the multi-verse.

"Stasis bubble holding steady, Captain," Arnold announced.

"Prepare to rotate out," the Captain ordered.

Arnold pushed the power to maximum, ready to initiate the virtual breach out of our universe into what some fondly called "subspace."

"Power at maximum, Captain. Ready to initiate breach," Arnold announced.

"Execute!"

There was a flash in my optic nerve, like seeing someone take a flash picture from the corner of my eye.

I'm Theodore Park, the documentarian for this historic flight, the person responsible for recording events during the mission. I'm responsible for the recordings from the dozen exterior cameras and the half dozen cameras recording what happens in the common crew areas of the Searcher. Our ship was financed by a conglomerate of the wealthiest technology companies in the world looking to spread their hegemony into every possible universe.

It was because of my two decade career as a respected science writer that I won the coveted documentarian spot on the crew and the competition despite my being Black. Some voices were raised over half of the crew being represented by African Americans by the pantheon of white network talking heads (yeah, I laughed at them). There were also objections to installing an empiricist as the mission documentarian, but for once, science won out over political expediency, and persistent racial prejudice. And, after eight weeks of training on the recording equipment installed on the Searcher and how to keep from killing myself and the rest of the crew in an emergency, I was certified to launch.

The theory behind the inter-dimensional (I/D) penetrating effect was discovered by a collaboration between scientists at the Jet Propulsion Laboratories and Cambridge University in England. M-theory suggested eleven dimensions in our universe, most as small as a quantum point and one large enough to supposedly be observable. But getting outside of our universe and into the quantum space between an infinite number of other universes was the goal of the Searcher's first mission.

The four of us, Captain Iona Babbage, Engineer Eric Arnold, Astrophysicist Nina Simpson and myself were the first crew to man the Searcher, and our departure from Earth's orbit was a big deal back home.

Our maiden voyage was designed to prove the results of years of mathematic and scientific research that went into creating the I/D Drive. Actually, the I/D Drive wasn't really a propulsion-type drive at all, it would only rotate the Searcher out of our universe into inter-dimensional space and hopefully return us intact.

"Report!" Captain Babbage called out. She looked the part of the expedition leader, intense blue eyes, sharp but pleasant features against a background of cocoa brown skin and wearing her ubiquitous mission cap. Even while we were training everyone subconsciously responded to her in a deferential manner, military and civilians alike. Her commanding attitude always made her appear taller than her trim, five foot, seven inch frame. Though coming from a media background, even I automatically responded to her as my superior. As far as I could tell she had mastered the art of command and wielded her voice like a finely honed tool.

"According to the log, the I/D Drive has rotated us out of normal space," Eric reported.

"I'm getting no readings from the instruments, Captain," Nina reported, clearly perplexed.

"Nothing?" Captain Babbage asked, disbelief in her voice.

"Nothing. No radiation, no atmosphere, no radio static, and as you all can feel, no gravity," Nina ran through the instrument readings again to make sure. "I say we retract the sun screen and see for ourselves what's out there."

"You're sure there's no radiation?" Eric asked. "What about something exotic? Is there any way we can tell?"

"There's no ionizing radiation. If there's something else that I can't pick up with the sensors, then we're just shit out of luck. But at least looking for ourselves should give us some clue because as far as the sensors are concerned there's absolutely nothing out there!" Nina said in frustration, a frown marring her normally smooth forehead.

The captain looked at me and asked, "What do your cameras show, Ted?"

"All the external cameras show unbroken blackness with absolutely no detail. I really can't tell if there's nothing out there or they have all simply malfunctioned. Maybe it was rotation out of our universe that did something to them. I'm with Nina on this, if there's no radiation the sensors can detect out there we may as well take a look," I said, just as curious as everyone else. I was praying for something, anything to be visible otherwise I would useless with nothing to record, nothing to describe.

Captain Babbage turned to the controls, reaching up to trigger the retraction of the forward windshield (why do we still call it a windshield in outer space, I wondered).

When the whine of the shield's motors began, we all watched as the top edge of the windshield retracted from the protective groove in the hull. As the shield cleared the bulkhead and exposed just a fraction of the window, light could be seen outside through the crack.

Captain Babbage stopped the shield from retracting any farther and turned to me again. "Something's not right! Ted, run the diagnostics on the cameras, because clearly there's something lit up outside."

"Running them again, stand by," I replied as I initiated the entire suite of diagnostics, even rotating several different filters in front of each camera. The forward two should have shown something of the light we could see through the slit between the sun shield and the bulkhead.

"Sorry, Captain. I've tried everything, I've still got nothing," I reported, looking at Nina and shrugging my shoulders.

Babbage sighed, her hand hovering over the sun screen control. "To hell with it. In for a penny, in for a pound," she said as she triggered the control to fully retract the screen.

As it lowered, and I could see what was outside the ship, I was confused. There was light outside, but even still, nothing was being recorded by the cameras at all. I even "rewound" the digital recording and played back from several cameras and there was absolutely nothing recorded but pitch blackness.

"Hey, wait a minute!" Eric exclaimed.

"What?" the captain immediately inquired, ready to raise the sun shield.

"Look! There's no shadow from the light out there!" he said, leaning close to the window and waving his hand.

He was right. The scene outside was of a white sameness in every direction, like being surrounded by milk, but no shadow was cast inside the ship when Eric raised his arm in front of the viewport.

There was no clue to the extent of the space around us. For all I could see, the whiteness could have been painted on the window except for the apparent bizarre brightness of the light.

"Hello," came a voice inside my head. The strangeness of hearing "someone" who normally would have sounded like my own voice in the middle of my own head was unnerving. The voice was sexless in timbre, but my brain somehow interpreted it as male.

"Did anyone else hear that?" I asked, my heart rate jumping.

"If you mean a 'hello,' I did," replied the captain.

"I must say, you are a persistently curious race," the voice said.

"Um, hello there to you too. Who are you?" Babbage said out loud.

"I have no name. I just am," came the reply in our heads.

"My name is Iona. And I am here with three others."

"This, I know."

"Okay then, where are you?" she asked.

"I am everywhere. Or perhaps to better explain, there is nowhere that I am not. That includes in your universe as well," said the voice, still coming from inside my head.

The rest of the crew was silent, all of them thinking the same thing. After a moment I spoke aloud, "Would you be the creator of our universe?"

"I am the creator of all universes."

"In our multiverse theory we postulate an infinite number of universes existing. Are you the creator of all those universes?" I asked.

"That is correct."

"Are all those other universes populated?" I couldn't help myself.

"They are."

"Every single one of them?" I asked in frank disbelief, although I can't say exactly why I didn't believe.

"As in your universe, every other universe is populated with more than one kind of life."

"If I may ask, is that intelligent life? In our universe I mean."

"Yes, millions upon millions of species. Some have come and gone, some have yet to mature. I admit that I am quite surprised that you traveled here, I didn't think you would last long enough to advance this far."

"Then you know of us?" Although I didn't quite know why I was surprised.

The humor was plainly evident in the voice inside my head. "I wouldn't be very good at this if I wasn't able to keep track of my creations, now would I? I monitor every single life in every single universe."

"Many of the people of our world imagine you as a supreme being, a God if you are familiar with the concept," I explained.

"I am quite familiar with your concept. However I fit the descriptions of a god in very few ways."

"You mean you're really not an omnipotent, god-like creature? If not, then why not?" I asked.

Now the feeling of amusement was very strong. "Your minds are not able to encompass the extent of what I am. All your visualizations of a god, as you put it, are manifestations of your own species, and are as stunted and as cognitively retarded as you are. Your gods are perverted constructs of men who use the idea to control others in your communities."

The feeling from the voice was now of profound sadness. "You have had many thousands of years to outgrow the need to dominate those around you for covetous gain or control, and yet you're no further along than you were when your species invented the concept of god. Up until right now there was no empirical proof to your kind that any form of a creator existed, and yet your species has spent thousands of years of insulting, fighting and killing over who has the best imaginary friend. And not a one of you can point to any societal gain for their belief other than greed, fear or persecution."

"But look how far we've come. We're here!" Captain Babbage interjected.

"So you are. This is by luck more so than by design. Had you asked me four billion years ago whether or not your species would have managed to arrive here before you destroyed yourselves, the odds would have been on it never happening. What do you believe was your intention in traveling here?"

We looked at each other, none of us quite sure how to answer. Finally, Nina took a shot at it. "We're here extending our reach from our birth planet. Investigating whether or not we can travel far and fast enough to find other intelligent life in our galaxy."

"What makes you think that anyone else in your galaxy would want to meet you? "

"You know of every life in our galaxy, in our universe even. Are you telling us that we wouldn't be welcomed by any other life form we would encounter?" I asked.

"The question you should be asking is: what is it about you that makes you believe you would be welcomed by anyone else? I have to admit that the arrogance of your species has been a source of sad amusement to me ever since you learned to communicate with each other."

"Arrogance?" Captain Babbage asked.

"That is correct," the voice said.

"How so?" I asked, desperately wanting clarification.

"In far too many ways. The fact that you would think a god cared in the least what you do in your daily lives is the height of arrogance. And to persecute those around you on the basis of them not acting in a manner that your man-made god approves is a completely heinous act. More people on your world have been killed in the name of religious persecution than any other cause. Your species has never had a legitimate excuse for having done so. There is no such god as you know it, and certainly no god that would have demanded the killing of others for non-belief."

"What about you? You fit so much of our concept of what a God is, proof of the thesis even if our concept of God only has some minuscule intersection with your actuality," I said. "There are too many similarities in the Talmud, the Bible and the Koran to discount out of hand our belief in God, and I believe, by extension, in you."

"Those works were written by men. Many were men of good conscience, but all of limited vision by their nature, their own self-interest. In all three works there is a lack of equality for women, for example. Is that really what a god would demand, that one sex have dominion over the other? That any god would truly play gender favorites?"

"Then how did the notion spread to all three works? Was there some historical reason for the status quo?" Nina asked.

"Obviously none of you realize that as recently as twenty-five thousand years ago women ruled every community on your planet. From the dawn of man's self-awareness the mysticism of woman raised their status above that of males for two reasons: they gave birth and they could bleed without dying. It was only when men invented organized religion was power wrestled away from women and came to rest in hands of men; women have suffered ever since. Please note that it is not my intention to inject my perspective into your species' gender politics, I merely make the observation.

"The truth is that what you do as a species and how you do it should never be of concern to a god because a true god, by definition, would not be concerned with the petty affairs of mortals. Sadly, the gods you have created are even more flawed than yourselves. More's the pity that your willful blindness prevents you from seeing it."

"Okay then, please answer me this," Eric began. "Did you know we were coming here?"

"I did."

"Then did you 'create' this place, because it appears to defy cosmological consistency and any notion of reality?"

"I did."

"Okay, why?" Eric asked.

"So that we may have this conversation."

We looked at each other, all of us wondering exactly what this conversation was really about, where it was going.

"And just why is that?" Babbage asked, uncertain, like the rest of us, whether or not she really wanted to hear the answer.

"You are here because you need to understand the fundamental truth of your existence."

"And that is?" Babbage asked.

"That this is the first and last time you will be allowed to travel outside of your universe."

"Why?" Babbage immediately asked.

"Because you will not be allowed to infect any other universe with your presence, and more importantly, your beliefs."

We were all shocked into silence.

A full minute later I stoked up the courage to ask, "Is that all?"

"And that you will be confined to your solar system from this time forward, again for the same reason."

"What have we done to deserve this isolation?" Eric asked.

"You have reached an evolutionary dead end."

Again, no one had any rebuttal or comment.

"Is there anything else?" I asked, afraid of the answer.

"That is more than enough, don't you agree?"

"But what about all the people throughout our history who have strived and sacrificed to try to bring humanity to a more enlightened existence?" I asked, pleading our case.

"And so? Is every person on your world celebrated as being as worthy as every other?"

I was immediately deflated, knowing exactly what the voice meant.

"You should be consoled that your isolation will not last for very long."

Everyone else was silent, but I had to ask. "Why is that?"

"You already know why."

"Can't you just tell us? Tell us how, and when it's going to happen?" Nina pleaded.

"That's entirely up to you."

"But you just said we were an evolutionary dead end. When does the end come?" Eric asked.

"Again, the end is up to you, but know that you have reached as far as you are going to advance as a species. Nothing conceptually has changed in your species in several millennia."

"Do you have any message for us to take back, something that might make a difference?" the captain inquired.

"And what might that message be? What could you say that would have any influence over your entire species, especially those who rule your world? As it is, none of you are going to be believed by the majority of your people once you return, are you?"

Babbage weakly laughed. "You're probably right."

"You are welcome to persist until they believe you, because you are confined to your own solar system."

"Forever?" I asked. "I mean there's no appeal? No possibility of parole?"

"It wouldn't matter," the voice said ominously

"Why not?" even I heard the desperation in my voice.

"Because no matter what you say, no one will truly believe this discussion took place. And more importantly, nothing will change. Do you really believe that your wealthy will stop soiling their own nest because of some enlightened message you bring home? That they will, somehow, come to the realization that everyone on your world is in the same boat?" There was silence, none of us having anything to say. "There is one other message you may want to try convey to the world when you get back."

"What is that?" Babbage got up the nerve to ask.

"Perhaps let your religious leaders know that I care not at all for any of their concerns, nor for anyone's actions on your world; I never have."

Suddenly I was blinded by a brilliant flash outside the spacecraft window and then when my eyes could finally focus, all I saw were stars through the viewport. We had returned to our own universe.

When we rendezvoused with our sister ship Pathfinder, stationed a thousand miles away as an observer, we were surprised to discover that from their perspective we hadn't left our universe at all. All subsequent activations of the I/D Drive yielded nothing, no rotation of either ship, Searcher or Pathfinder, occurred. Nina swore that according to her instruments two very important cosmological constants were different from before we left, those changes invalidating the underlying principles of the I/D Drive. Unfortunately she couldn't find any sign in the onboard scientific literature of any such change, all reference materials agreed with the universe's current cosmological attributes. According to our data banks the current cosmological constants had always been this way.

The hardest fact for me to face about our trip to the other side was that the human race was doomed to extinction; the only question was when. Knowing that our universe was full of life, dead and gone, completely out of our reach, or not scheduled to reach its full potential for centuries, perhaps millions or billions of years to come was a bitter pill for me to swallow. And the voice was right, no one believed a word of it when we returned to Earth.

The four of us were separated and interrogated, even under drugs, and all our stories matched to the exact words we reported hearing in our heads. The Searcher's cameras had recorded nothing. The computers were wiped, as was the flight recorder as if we hadn't left; an act beyond any crew member's capability. And though the data recorders were specifically designed so that no amount of tampering on our part could delete or corrupt the information stored, the government spooks accused me of having done just that. Their interrogation methods were harsh and left me confused, dopey with fatigue behind the clinical effects of whatever drugs they used on me. They refused to believe what any of us reported, and for a while I was convinced we were just going to disappear, but then something happened.

Someone leaked the videos of our interrogation, specifically the parts where we recounted the conversation we had with the voice on the other side. At first the government denied the veracity of the recordings and transcripts, but all too soon their denials fell apart. I was sure we were going to be killed so that the reports would have no real attribution, no substantiation with none of us available as proof. Then the government could stonewall forever, knowing eventually the furor would die for lack of traction.

I had already made peace with myself since obviously there was no one else to appeal to. There was no God as we knew it, and the only entity who could conceivably serve in that capacity had told us in no uncertain terms that it was completely unconcerned with the affairs of man.

After several months the government finally cut us loose, forcing the four of us to sign non-disclosure statements that were essentially promissory notes reminding us of exactly the dominion they held over as long as each of us should live.

Once we resurfaced we were mobbed by the public. We had no peace. But we all kept our silence. I kept silent, never speaking a word of what went on when we were on the other side to anyone, especially family and friends.

Ambush interviews, even those where the person or persons played back our own words to us under interrogation were met with stoic silence creating a cottage industry of conspiracy theories.

I was told Eric tried to privately convince the Cardinal of his church about what the voice said on the other side once he returned home, but it was a worthless effort. Religious doctrine being what it was, no amount of reality would ever shape belief.

Surprisingly, Eric was brought to the Holy See for a private audience with the Pope. No one was privy to the content of the conversation between the two, but Eric's return home without official comment from the Vatican was telling in itself.

Sects of Non-Believers grew around the world, formed because of our recounting of the conversation we had on the other side. Against our will the four of us were worshiped as disciples of an uncaring entity, an entity that was the creator of all things, with all the attributes of a God but with none of the attendant evil man ascribes to his flawed understanding. Deities were man's construct in every organized religion in every culture by necessity, but now there was a growing backlash.

Religious conservatives were in retreat as a growing movement fed up with small-minded people dictating culture and law based on what was called, history's longest running lie, or at best, delusion in the history of man's civilization began to amass significant numbers. The movement gained more and more followers everywhere, while religious conservatives and zealots were ignored, ridiculed and attacked for their historical deprivations, their creation of pariahs, their past murders, and genocides.

Life didn't change much for me, maybe there was a little more tiptoeing around me by others in matters about the mission. The most disturbing issue that rose and then fell just as quickly was the accusation that the captain and I were some kind of Black Power devotees bent on destroying Christianity or the underpinnings of white society. All-in-all, nothing came of that bullshit notion, although my Methodist family never really treated me the same.

I returned to my media job as a freelance technical writer, more often than not using a pseudonym to avoid controversy, and frankly, to get paid. I grew a beard with entirely too much gray for my taste, changed from wearing contact lenses back to glasses, even moved to a new address. Eventually, pretty much no one was looking for me anymore, but I never forgot the profound change the mission made in me.

These days I'm seeing something that gives me hope, something that just might be bringing some sanity to the world. My secret hope is that this growing trend might just make the entity we met on the other side change its mind about our world's isolation.

What's bringing me hope is this movement making its way around the globe, something perhaps suggesting an unexpected maturity in our species encapsulated in the slogan of the movement:
"HE *never* cared."

ARTIFACTS

Kelly King

Prologue – 60 Years Ago

Captain Tan Rogers raced to the Communications room. The aft drive had been compromised and the backend of the ship started collapsing in around itself. Something with a very strong gravitational force had pulled the artificial blackhole out of its containment field. The ship's system couldn't react fast enough to correct the problem, thus dooming the ship to disaster. Rogers called breathlessly for Mr. Piper as he ran into the room. A young man with sandy brown hair and a pale complexion looked up. Fear was written all over his face. He swallowed hard as the ship started an approximate of listing. The overhead lights had turned amber minutes ago and the klaxon alarm was a constant reminder that death was near.

"Yes, sir!" Piper said.

Rogers handed the young man a note. "Send this tight beam to Command Proper Priority Omega. Place it in a loop and head to the nearest escape pod."

The young man accepted the note with sweaty palms and nodded. This was it. He read it and understood. Up until now the mission had been a bust, but this would ensure some hope of rescue. "I'm on it, sir."

Rogers nodded and left. A lump formed in the back of his throat. He headed back to the command center. Once he entered the command deck he said, "Sound-Abandon ship." He sat at the pilot's station. "Densel," he said over the klaxon. "Godspeed."

The first officer stood next to Rogers. "Sir, it wasn't your fault."

"I know, but . . . this is my ship." Tears welled up in his eyes. "Besides, someone has to stir the McCain away from the pods."

Densel hesitated.

Rogers looked up into his first officer's eyes. "Antonio, please. Martha and the kids are waiting for you. They . . ."

"May never know." Densel finished.

"Antonio, please. Take the chance. Please."

The first officer squeezed the shoulder of his Captain. Then without warning he embraced him in a strong hug.

Rogers gave him an equally strong embrace. "Give Martha and my grandkids my love."

Densel nodded. Wiped his eyes and ran to the waiting Command Escape Pod. The rest of the Bridge crew were secured and silent." Densel looked back one last time to see his Captain strap in.

Rogers wiped the tears from his eyes as he clicked into the pilot's seat. He monitored the distance to the closest pods. Eighty were still attached to the hull. He pressed the Ship Intercom button. "All hands, all hands. This is the Captain speaking. I am releasing all remaining pods in sixty seconds. Hurry."

Densel secured himself in the command chair and pressed the release. A second later he felt the downward push of acceleration as the escape pod distanced itself from the McCain. He switched on the main overhead viewer, giving everyone on board a look at the McCain as dozens of little and large cylindrical objects sped away. When the last of the pods were released the McCain's aft was already a shrinking mass of knotted metal. With each second it got smaller and smaller.

Rogers had to override the ship's safety protocol to gain control over the bow engine. He pulled on the Nav stick and instructed the computer to begin emergency phase forward motion. Some of the closer escape pods might get sucked back into the ship's gravity wake but it couldn't be helped. He needed the McCain to be at least a hundred thousand kilometers away from the bulk of the escape pods before he destructed the ship. The acceleration pushed him further in the pilot's chair. "It dies with the McCain," he whispered as he entered the destruct code.

Densel watched the monitor intensely. The McCain was still

broadcasting its Mayday. A message that was partly true, yet partly a lie. He clicked on the audio and piped it on the speakers. "Mayday, Mayday," He heard Lt. Piper's voice. "This is the McCain. Engine failure by heavy gravity anomaly 30 light-years away. Not there before. Request rescue. Artifacts found on planet surface. Repeat. Artifacts found on planet surface."

His home of over ten years was crumpling before his eyes. Thirty minutes and a hundred kilos away later the hull buckled and the ship started to horseshoe. He wiped at a tear running down his cheek. "Gonna miss you, McCain."

Then in a flash of brilliant white light the McCain was gone. A minute later the escape pod was hit with the shockwave and tossed out past a low planetary orbit into deep space. The alarms sounded and the pod lost main power. Battery reserves kicked in and the pod was flooded with amber light. The inertial field re-engaged, flickered, then held. Densel felt like his stomach yanked against his ribs. He heard the unsettling but familiar sound of several crew members throwing up. Thank Goddess the pod maintained some gravity and kept the mess on the floor. A few moments later the pod stopped accelerating. Densel tapped at the middle LED panel at his side. He instructed the pod to maintain an orbit around the planet. Once the computer beeped an acknowledgement Densel settled himself in for a long surreal wait. He sent out a wide spectrum broadcast requesting all pods to report in to him.

The pod had a total of four sections and was capable of sustaining them for five years at normal rations. It was equipped with four medical stasis beds and six crew stasis chambers. The top section was command and control. The second section was the sleep area. The third was the galley and living area with the fourth being used for storage, suits, tools, and supplies. There were twelve in the pod. Densel ran the numbers through his head. Ten asleep, two awake, for five years. If that soon. No one injured. That was a plus. Seven women, five males. Two gay males and five lesbian females with two of the females rumored bisexual. Pretty much everyone liked each other. That was a plus, because, now they would be in this Pod for three years. Maybe more. The message went out Quantum Assist, which meant Earth would be getting the message in several days. It'll take the Alliance a year to send a rescue, of which may take two, three, four, or five years to reach them. They were in for the long haul and had no choice. "Is everyone okay," he finally said aloud. He received nods. No doubt they all went through some mental calculations and came to, hopefully, a similar conclusion. They were fucked, but not by that much. He checked the inventory for several things: Birth-control pills. Plenty. Grog? About three years at 750 ml for four members per day. And weapons. Two low velocity impact pistols. The computer had already identified him as Pod Commander, so his thumb print and voice command would allow him to fire the weapons. The second pistol was locked until he instructed the computer otherwise. He tapped at his chair LED and read all the pods that had reported in. He activated a locator pulse and noted the nearest pods. Twelve within 50 kilometers. Fifty at more than 100 and the rest out passed 1200. He was now the Fleet Commander to a hundred tiny vessels floating in space. The biggest smallest fleet this side of the galaxy. "I'm hungry," he said while unsnapping his harness. "I think we should eat before we settle in for a long, long, long, wait."

Several females and one male had been crying. The scene of the McCain crumpling, then exploding had been a bit much. Some wiped their eyes and nodded. Densel heard a collective unsnapping of harnesses. And thus, hour one began.

Chapter 1

Lieutenant Commander Wayne Piper woke up covered in sweat. He had the night terrors again. The fifth night in a row and he was beginning to worry. He had stopped remembering the nightmares for years, but lately the same two kept recurring. The drug Klonopin, was an old one, but mostly effective. At least until a few days ago. Tonight was different though. He woke himself up because on his screaming. This particular terror didn't have anything to do with fear. No, not this one he thought. This was more like guilt and shame and realizing he could have done something different. But, the question arose, what? He sighed deeply and rolled over. After a moment he realized it was worthless. The sheets were too wet to get comfortable. Dread seemed to consume his body and left him too exhausted to sleep. "Lights on," he said as he got out of bed and walked into the bathroom.

It had been about twenty years since the crew of the McCain had been rescued. Forty years after the ship sent out a Mayday – 37 years too long. All active rescues during the initial stage of the war had been halted, thus everyone he knew was dead or dying when he got back to Earth. He looked in the mirror and saw too many wrinkles. His eyes were puffy and his frown lines were deep. The crow's feet at the corner of each eye gave him some satisfaction. He could say they were from laughing at life often, instead of being bitter. The face in the mirror slowly shook its head. "You only laugh at life when you are conscious." He said out loud.

Stepping out of the bathroom he walked over to his desk and checked his messages. GRID Central sent him a Vid message. He sat down behind the computer and opened it.

"All is well, Commander." His boss, Admiral Ty said. "I have one last mission for you. It's a cold-case that shouldn't take long for you to solve."

Piper was set to retire in a month. He laughed. The Admiral said it shouldn't take too long. He was good at his job, but a month? The Admiral had too much confidence in his abilities. Piper considered himself an excellent Investigator. He was thorough with his investigations. He'd eliminate all that was possible and whatever evidence was left, no matter how improbably it related to the case, it had to be the truth. He solved 93% of his cases, and that was good. The other 7% had enough evidence for him to finger the prep, but not enough to bring to trial. Or, in some cases, had been swept aside. The Most High Goddess was pretty influential. It didn't help that he, too, was a follower and sometimes there were cases of ethical violations, but he did the best he could in finding a balance between the two. In the most extreme cases, he would hand all his evidences to a follow Investigator and let them do the arrest. He had enough accolades to last several lifetimes.

". . . Meet me in my office first thing in the morning. Have a good evening." The video blinked off.

Piper scratched his forehead. 'A cold-case', he thought. Not unexpected, but Ty always knew how to bait and hook him. The last cold-case took eight months to finish but it ended in a conviction of a member of a local parliament. It was a shame, and Piper felt bad – only for a minute, but the crime was horrendous and justice had to be served. He tapped the local news and skimmed through the usual headlines: "SI War takes another turn", "Colonists saved from the SI", "Colonists lost by the SI", "GRID Central has an ambitious plan", and on and on and on. It was the war that delayed the McCain rescue. Piper switched the news off and tapped out the code to open his personal files. A picture of Wendy Gordon, crewmate and friend from the McCain, brightly smiled. She was in uniform and looked lovely. Piper smiled and tried to dredge up past memories. Almost nothing came up. He knew he liked Wendy, and he "knew" she liked him. He figured. The Doctor's said it was Brain Tissue damage from a combination of drugs, alcohol, and the stasis process. Even hypnosis turned up very little. During one session he displayed unexplainable rage toward Blifford "Bliff" Kingslayer. Earthside records classified Bliff as a life-long friend. They went through the Academy together, served on the Norton, Mandela, and the McCain. So, it was odd why he had such a strong reaction whenever Bliff's name was mentioned. He rubbed his forehead and scratched at the side of his head. In another three hours the Admiral would be up.

Piper washed up and dressed. He decided to head into work early. It wasn't like he had retirement plans already worked out. He didn't. Retirement really wasn't something he wanted to do, nor had he thought it completely through. He just thought that one day a bad guy would gun him down and that would be that. "Computer, secure mode, please." He said as he walked out the front door. Just before it closed he heard the computer's three tone beeps.

***

Ty sat at his desk staring at the McCain artifact – The Box. The original four corner C-clamps were still locked and the last attempt to crack the code was done ten years ago. When it was discovered it brought out more questions than answers. It was a secret about a secret and no one knew what the original secret was. Ty looked over the hardcopy data sheets about The Box. Just before the McCain imploded the Captain, Tan Rogers, sent out a Mayday. The McCain's aft engine had breached its protective wall and doomed the ship. Half the crew survived in Escape Pods because Captain Rogers was able to move the ship to a safe distance before it imploded. The Box was found on board the Command Escape Pod – all personnel dead, through sabotage. Cameras and Audio pickup had been disabled. The Medical Escape Pod had damage. The entire medical staff killed because of a hull breach. Those personnel rescued reported that Commander Densel was in charge, then some hours later Lt. Commander Kingslayer reported that the Commander had an accident and all of Medical Staff was lost. After that he told personnel to initiate Stasis and start fireguard watch on the larger Escape Pods. The mystery was that Commander Densel and Lt. Commander Kingslayer were both missing. Forensics placed both in the Command Escape Pod as well as, at the time, Lt. Piper. Yet Piper, upon rescue was in a single Escape Pod and couldn't remember a single thing about the accident. His system was pumped full of drugs whose side effects were amnesia. The Medical Examiner at the time said Piper was lucky he hadn't lost all memory. Apparently, he entered stasis as the drugs just started to take effect, thus minimizing complete and utter memory loss.

Ty reached out and touched one of the C-clamps. Piper's fingerprints had covered every single clamp. His prints and DNA were on the surface of most of The Box, yet he, in a written statement, couldn't remember The Box. He didn't remember the combinations nor being on the Command Escape Pod. A Psyche scan verified he was telling the truth. After several months of investigating and questioning, all the evidence had been collected, catalogued, and shelved – for twenty years, until now. Ty looked over to his wall clock. It would be 0400 in another three minutes and he expected Piper to be at his desk reading over his last assignment, The Box. Then he heard a knock at his door. "Enter."

Piper stepped through. "Sir, morning. I hadn't expected you here this early. Chuck said you've been here for hours."

Ty smiled. "Yeah." He gestured toward a chair next to his desk. "Have a seat."

Piper started walking to the chair when he noticed The Box. He paused for a moment, then continued. He sat in the chair, staring at The Box the entire time. It featured prominently in all his nightmares. He remembered being questioned endlessly about it, but he could never remember any useful details about it. Then a Psyche Eval cleared him and he was allowed to continue serving in the service. "Is this my cold-case?"

Ty nodded. "Partially." He pushed a folder filled with notes, photos, and documents. Autopsies were included.

Piper took it and leafed through the contents. After a few moments he said, "One month? Really, Boss."

Ty reacted with a large grin. "It's a cold-case. It doesn't require resolution in that time, just some forward movement. The Council found another box and would like to know of any connection."

Piper blinked several times. "Movement?"

Ty nodded. "Are they related? The two boxes? The one we found at location Zed 45 Eta 10 seems older but is carved in a more artistic manner. This box is surprisingly simple compared to the second one. Plus, the newly discovered box is not sealed."

Piper nodded. "Just forward movement? What was found in this second box?"

"Just forward movement. No need to resolve the actual mystery but see if there is a connection. And, the second box had three rings made of different material. And a wand of sorts. We have no idea, yet, how to read the writings inside the second box, but we are certain the languages in either box are completely different."

Piper nodded. Damn you he thought. "Rings – and a wand? As in magic wand?"

Ty slowly nodded. "The council nearly orgasmed –"

"I bet!"

". . . Our Most High wants to dispatch a ship out there, but . . ."

Piper nodded, "The war."

"So, whatever info you can dig up the better."

Piper stared at The Box for a long moment. "I don't remember much, you know that?"

Ty nodded. "I do."

"And, I may not come up with anything, you know that too?"

"Of course, but you and I know you like a challenge." Ty got up from his chair and walked to a small upright cooler set in a corner of the office. He opened the door and pulled out two bottles of Adult beverage. Walking back to his desk he handed one to Piper.

"So early?"

"So late. I've been here since yesterday." He pulled the tab off the top and took a sip.

Piper followed. The liquid slid down his throat smoothly. He liked Ty's choice of booze. "I don't know?"

Ty smiled. "What are you afraid of? We've known each other for a long time."

Piper nodded and took a swallow.

"It's only The Box . . ."

"That started an earnest effort of finding other artifacts."

"The second box."

"Why me?" Piper asked

"Retirement, my friend, retirement. Officially, you are on the backslid to doing nothing, but you now have nearly unlimited time and resources at your disposal . . ." He held up a finger. "All your other cases have been reassigned. This is from GRID Central and the Most

High Council."

"The Most High? A month?"

Ty shrugged. "The timeframe is up to you. After retirement The Most High may want you in her circle." He slid The Box closer to Piper. "Your finger prints. Must be your combination."

Piper stared at the box. Dread gripped his heart. One month he said. One month. "Or I tried and failed numerous times."

Ty shrugged. "Your prints. Today it's not my problem. It's surprisingly light."

Piper took the clue. His time was up and it was time to go. He lifted The Box up and agreed. It was surprisingly light. When he reached the door he looked back. Ty was already staring at a PAAD. He gave a wave. Piper nodded and headed to his desk. A month. And the Most High was watching.

Piper placed The Box on top his Desk. The four C-clamps looked like robotic legs. He lifted his PAAD and tapped out his passcode. He placed it back on the Desk as the device projected a black sphere a meter above its surface. "Wen," he began, "What do we know about The Box?"

A mezzo-soprano female voice said, "Evidential or Incidental?"

Piper pondered a moment. Every time he heard Wen's voice it reminded him of Gordon. He specifically programmed his PAAD to sound like her. At first the Doctors' were worried of his obsession, but after a time they agreed the end results did justify the means to recovery. He had been allowed to pursue a career change from Communications to Adjutant Investigative Branch. "Evidential, please."

Wen said, "The Box has an Isotopic Analysis date of approximately 1200 years. It has a dimension of 0.5 meters long, 24 centimeters high, and 24 centimeters wide. It weighs 5 kg. Inside is depleted Uranium lined. X-rays have given negative results. There is a formula written along the edge on The Box lid . . ."

"Wait? What?"

"Wayne, there is a formula written along the edge on The Box's lid."

"Show me, please."

Wen replaced the sphere with floating characters.

Some Piper thought he recognized, but of course he felt that was impossible. Maybe. One symbol looked like an upside-down pi, another was three short wavy lines one on top another. He thought Hieroglyph. There was a square at the very end. "Okay, Wen, no one has cracked the code in twenty years. I don't think we'll do it in a day."

"Done."

Piper said, "What? Done, what?"

Wen replied, "Wayne, you've used those symbols before . . ."

"Impossible!"

The display changed to an image of a document. It was titled "Encryptions by Deception." The author was Lieutenant Wayne Piper, published during AIT.

Piper frowned. "I don't remember that. And, besides. Wouldn't the best and brightest in GRID have looked at that already?"

"Records show that it was mentioned, and tried, but shelved. Arrogance, Wayne, still lives."

"Why?"

"At the time, no one took your ideas seriously."

Piper laughed. "Okay, smart ass, what's the combination to each clamp?"

"36 – 42 – 78 – 15, starting with the right-side clamp facing the front."

"There's six places for the combo. Why only two digits –"

"The first set takes up the first two spots. For the second clamp enter the number starting in the second spot. The third clamp, enter the number starting at the third spot, and the last clamp enter the number starting in spot four."

Piper hesitated. "How did you figure it out so quickly?"

"I hadn't. I've been working on it for the last five years."

"Seriously? Five years?" Piper said incredulously.

"Wayne. If it doesn't work we can try something else."

Piper nodded. Wen was right. She almost was always right. "What are you going to do when I retire?"

"What we always do. You won't stay idle. You can't."

He stared at The Box.

Wen said, "Wayne, try the combinations."

"Wen, if the combos work that means I'm part of this entire mystery."

"And the problem lies where?"

Piper finally concluded that he and Wen were married. "I don't want to be part of the mystery."

"And?"

He frowned. "And, I am scared."

"Noted. Now, please, try the combinations."

Piper reached out and entered the first number.

Nothing.

He exhaled and smiled. "Ha!"

"Place your thumb on the biosensor plate."

"Wait, what?"

"The biosensor plate. On top of each clamp."

Piper hovered his thumb over the spot. If the clamp unlocked then his soul was doomed to damnation. He pressed down.

The clamp went 'Thunk' loudly and dread washed over Piper. He had committed himself.

"I'm fucked." He said out loud.

"Try the other three clamps before you doom yourself to hell."

Piper swallowed hard. The other three clamps unlocked. "Fuck, fuck, fuck." He paused. "Shouldn't I be doing this in some secured location? Just in case I release some toxic germ?"

"The Box is not airtight enough to contain a sterile environment. It's been subjected to twenty years of analysis. It is safe."

Piper removed each clamp. The Box rested in front of him.

Wen said, "Remove the lid."

Transfixed, Piper broke the spell. "Huh? The lid, of course." He reached out and grabbed a corner. He lifted it up gingerly at first. A few seconds later he removed the lid altogether.

"Interesting." Wen said.

"What?" He peered into The Box. A dozen items rested neatly inside it. Then he frowned. "What the - ?"

"Wayne, this is not good."

He leaned back into his chair. "It's . . . it's . . ."

Wen finished, ". . . junk."

"Junk!"

"Wayne, I just said that."

Piper took a deep breath. "Junk! Wen, send what we have so far to Ty."

"Done."

Piper nodded. If Ty had any reservations he'd given him a chance to voice them early. "This picture 'feels' familiar." He pulled out an image of what looked like an alien. It was embedded in a metal plate and had a slightly low opacity.

"It is. The image is about 95% likeness of a very popular First

Shooter Game during the early 21st century."

Piper's frown deepened. There were several stone tiles with scribble on them. Clearly, they were fake. His cheeks reddened. "What was I going to accomplish with this?"

Wen said, "We have data from the other Escape Pods."

"Such as?" Piper rubbed at the stubble underneath his chin.

"Nanocleaner video."

He stopped rubbing. "Nanocleaners?"

"Only three thousand and thirty survived. The original investigative team collected all the Nanocleaners they could find and put them in storage. Only the three thousand and so have survived. During the investigation they were able to create several holographic scenes."

Wen had Piper's attention now. "What was the conclusion?"

"A few murders."

Piper blinked several times. "I was never told that."

Wen said, "As you should not have been told. You were a suspect."

"I'm not liking this one bit."

"Wayne, apparently, you were cleared. You're here investigating a cold-case instead of being in jail or . . ."

Piper nodded, ". . . 2 meters under? True. Are the holographic builds available?"

Wen paused a long moment.

Piper asked, "Wen, what's wrong? You almost never hesitate."

Wen remained silent.

"Wen, give. We've known each other too long."

"Wayne, it's not good. Some of the scenes had been extrapolated from circumstantial evidence. So, it may have or have not happened exactly on that day."

"I'm getting the impression this is not a cold case."

"Analysis indicates the same . . ."

"Analysis? Wen! You're spooked."

"Wayne . . . I am concerned."

Piper let that sink in. Wen had been concerned maybe two or three times through the two decades they've known each other. Each time it was life threatening. The last time, about eight years ago, Wayne nearly lost his legs. He got the bad guys, but the price was high. His legs were saved, but at the cost of his soul . . . to The Most High Goddess. "I want to see."

Silence.

"Wen . . . ?"

"Wayne, arrangements have been made. We'll have to go to the one of the GraphView rooms in the Boehner McConnell Hall . . ."

Piper raised an eyebrow. "It's that long?"

"Yes, over several petabytes and protected under the seal of The Most High."

Piper frowned. "That's a bit extreme."

"I've already seen it . . . and there is something else."

"Yes?"

"The items in The Box were not all junk."

"Wait, what?"

"There's something missing."

"Like?"

"A wand . . . kind of."

Piper cocked his head to one side, "A wand? As in magic wand?"

"As in a possible weapon in the shape of a wand."

Deep in thought Piper finally said, "Interesting. So that means The Box had been opened before?"

"From what is shown in the holoscene and what is not in The Box I would conclude yes."

"Would Ty know this Box was opened before?"

"Inconclusive. Are you giving me a probable cause?"

"We can't look at Ty's email. That's invasion of privacy."

"Wayne, you want answers the easy way, or the tedious hard way?"

That raised an interesting question. "Wen, send a formal request to Admiral Ty's office on want my limitations are in gathering evidence."

"Done. I also added a formal request for jurisdictions classifications."

Piper nodded. Would Ty allow him to search through The Most High records?

"Wayne, we have a reply."

"So, soon?"

Wen said, "Very interesting."

"What's that?"

"Besides getting a response back this quickly, Admiral Ty preemptively sent you an encrypted file."

"It was sent as an auto-reply?"

"Apparently. Wayne, I think you should see the holoscenes. Authorization has already been given."

"What about the encrypted file?"

"I can't crack it . . . yet."

"I'm not going to like what I see, will I?"

"On more than one level, no."

Piper felt like he was hit with cold water. 'On more than one level, no.' He sighed and got up. He grabbed Wen and headed out the door. Face your fears they say. Look fear in the eye they say. Screw them he thought.

Chapter 2

Densel surveyed the group. All twelve crowded in the third level living area. This level served as the dining, meeting, and recreational area. A large circular table was placed in the center. Multiple screens were aligned along the walls and three 80 cm monitors were secured at the center of the table forming a triangle. "It's gonna probably take four years before we get help." Densel said.

Steward, the ship's secondary pilot nodded. He was a soft spoken male with brown hair, green eyes, and a fey build. He said, "Agreed. Earth will get the McCain's Mayday within the next 120 hours. It'll probably take another three months if not more to reallocate resources. It took five years to rescue the crew from the Romney, and they were 40 light-years closer to Earth."

Gordon cleared her throat. She had blond hair and was by ship's consensus the prettiest of all the female crew. She was also firmly gay and probably going to be the most difficult. She loved pushing buttons and being aggressive during discussions. "But that was ten years ago. ComProp has since then streamlined rescue. Two years, tops."

Steward shook his head. "I don't think so. The McCain is not a line ship with no VIPs on board. We . . ."

"Please!" Gordon interrupted. "ComProp will push hard."

"Ha! That's right. The Fleet Admiral's daughter." Steward quipped.

"And, so? Maybe that's a good thing for us."

Densel watched in near panic.

Steward frowned. "Or, maybe the worse thing."

"What do you mean?" Gordon asked.

"The Old Man may not want to be seen soft on his little princess." He wiggled his little finger. "Three years, minimum and . . ."

Gordon shouted, "Let's hope not! This boat is already too small." She wheeled on Densel. "Okay, sir. What do you have to say?"

Densel swallowed hard. Three years he thought. Three goddamn years. "I say we eat first. Clearly we have a long wait. We'll need to work out rotation, duties, and responsibilities."

"But, sir. Do you think it'll be three years or two?"

Densel stared into Gordon's eyes. They started to tear up and he realized she was afraid. He looked at the others and most had the same look. Fear, some anger, some horror, some shutdown completely. Those he couldn't read and that was scary. Honestly, Densel felt it would be closer to six. Steward hit the nail on the head. The Old Man would show concern, of course, but he would not divert trillions of dollars to rescue his daughter any faster than he would someone else's daughter. No, he'd go by the book. He'd have ComProp send a ship already in space. It would be a miracle if a ship were on this side of Earth, mostly not. That ship would have to stop mid mission and work out the details to head for the McCain's crew. That would add another five to ten years on their duty enlistment – whatever years it took to reach the pods and the time to return to Earth, if they did at all. ComProp may just order the ship to continue its original mission, which would add even more years to all crew involved. "It'll take as long as it'll take. Let's wait until ComProp responds before we lay bets." He could tell it wasn't good enough for some.

Steward nodded. "I'll shut my mouth until word gets here."

Gordon bit the bottom of her lip, but said nothing. She gave Steward the evil eye and found an empty seat and sat.

Densel made eye contact with Geb, one of the McCain's navigators. He motioned her over.

"Yes, sir?" She said.

"Geb, help me pass out some rations, please."

She nodded and made her way over to the galley.

Densel could hear fragmented conversations. He gathered a handful of food bags and walked them over to the table. Small groups had already started forming, which, Densel thought made it easier to decide who's on any given rotation watch. He decided he'd gather all the pods around the medical, it was the largest with eight sections and twice as wide as the command pod. The Command pod would be attached on top and the Engineer pod attached at the bottom. He located several security pods, which was good. He'd have those link up with medical.

While eating lunch he used the Table's main monitors and top surface keypad to identify all the pods. There was a total of one hundred and two pods. Sixty were emergency crew pods – those had the most personnel. About thirty each. He located the Galley Pod, which was good. It had RationTabs for a thousand crew for ten years. All together fifteen hundred survived. Densel keyed in the override command code and instructed all the Pods' main computer system to home in on his mark. He sent out a text broadcast requesting number of injured. Moments later responses started trickling in. Twelve pods had at least one person near critical, another two dozen with broken bones, three with non-life-threatening, for the time being, cuts. He instructed those pods to dock with medical first. All other pods would be within three hundred meters of one another. He looked up to vacant stares. Denial was starting to settle in. "Any one up for some Grog?" He asked. All hands went up. Densel smiled and walked over to the Spirit locker. He pulled out twelve small boxes of Grog and handed them out. He sat down, pierced the top with his fingernail and raised the box up in a toast. Serious or not serious he wondered. "Guys, we have each other now. Let's make this work. Up to our lips, past the gums, look out stomach, salvation comes."

The small group sat silent for a moment then the trickle of laughter filled the Pod. At least we have that, Densel thought. Everyone was on their third rations of Grog when Densel felt the first bump. The Med pod had locked in. He got up and went over to the airlock. He entered the cycle code and peered through the small porthole. A minute later his airlock door hissed open with a small pop. He crossed the lock gang boot and waited. After another minute he entered the emergency door override code. The system blinked green for 'all clear' and the door hissed and a small pop told him the pressure matched. He opened the door, stepped in and saw no one. The first level was empty. He stepped up to the ladder and made his way down to the main patient area. No one. All beds were empty. Densel went down to the living area. Again, not a soul. He made his way up to the command deck and found the hatch door locked. He peered through the tiny porthole and took in a sharp breath. A dozen bodies sat motionless in their chairs.

Bermudez, one of the McCain's navigators, walked up behind Densel. "Sir?"

Densel turned away, shaken. "The medical staff. Gone." He stepped aside.

Bermudez looked through the window. It seemed unusually bright. He was able to make out the edge of a large rip in the top half of the pod. Decompressor was immediate, no one had a chance. "We're screwed aren't we, sir?" The first officer's stoic expression made the young man nervous. Sir?"

Densel said nothing. His mind raced through doomsday scenarios, of which this was one. "Not quite. You remember your Med Training?"

"Some?"

"You're the new Med Chief until we find someone with more experience."

"What?!"

"Your luck in following me." Densel turned to the now clearly frightened man and smiled. "The odds are good that your new title will last until the next pod docks in."

Bermudez frowned. Not good he thought. 'I'm screwed from here to hell.'

Densel turned and made his way back down the access way to the airlock. He crossed the threshold . . .

Turner, one of the McCain's Engineers, spotted Densel first. "Not good." He said.

Densel said, "You say that not as a question?"

Turner nodded, "I don't see any Med staff behind you."

Bermudez nodded.

Densel heard someone ask, "What happened?"

"Looks like it was a hull breach. Decompression took them out quickly."

Gordon's eyes welled up in tears. Several other Pod mates turned with face buried in hands.

"Anyone with Med Training?" Densel asked.

"Yes." Gordon volunteered.

Densel turned to Bermudez, "You are relieved as Med Chief. You're Med Second." He looked Gordon in the eye, "Gordon, you are Med Chief. Most likely the entire Med Staff is gone. Hopefully, a few were off-duty and elsewhere when the order to abandon was announced." He shook his head. "I really am hoping some of them did not make it to the pod."

Bermudez amused, "Then some of them could be out with crew?"

Densel nodded. "You two are it for the moment. As pods get near we'll either add to staff or replace titles. Any problems?"

Both shook their heads.

"Good. How about another cup of Grog? It'll be another four hours before one of the Security Pods docks. And another ten hours before any on the Emergency Personnel Pods reach us. We can get some sleep." He surveyed the room. All scared. "People, we can do this. Once we've established a Connect and Secure with all the pods we can think about Stasis Rotation."

Some expressions eased from fear to anticipation.

McDonalds, from Environment, asked, "Do you really think we'll be rescued anytime soon?"

Densel faced the small man. He had dark eyes and dark hair. His skin was mocha. "After hearing the McCain's mayday message, ComProp just may speed things up."

Steward said, "But we didn't find any Alien artifacts."

Densel shrugged, "Captain's message. Not ours. But maybe that was what the Old Man was thinking. Instead of getting rescued in ten years it might be one or two."

Gordon gave Steward a smirk.

Steward chose to ignore it.

"We got about a week before we get word and I'd like to have all pods positioned and set with Stasis Rotation in place."

A second later there was a bump.

"What the . . . ?" Densel quickly moved up the ladder to the Command Section. He sat in his chair and keyed through the computer system. "The bottom airlock." He said as he hurried down the ladder to the fourth and last level. Steward, Gordon, McDonalds and others followed. He keyed in the door code and everyone entered. Stacks of alloyed boxes were against the wall in columns that went from floor to ceiling. The Airlock entry indicator remained red. Densel walked up to it and tapped at the touch screen next to the door. A single person escape pod had docked. The screen indicated that the occupant on the other side was alive and was ready to enter. Densel tapped out the entry cycle and stepped back. Moments later the door made a hiss pop sound.

Lt. Piper, holding what looked to be a medium sized stone box stepped out. There were four Security C –clamps on each of the long sides of the box.

"Piper!" Densel exclaimed! "Now I am surprised."

"Hey, Commander. Didn't think I was going to make it. Life-support failed after the McCain exploded."

Densel nodded. The pod must have been hit with debris. "And the box?"

Piper sucked in both lips. "Something important."

Densel nodded and gave the young man a squinted eye stare. "Later then."

Relieved, Piper exhaled. "Permission to come aboard, sir?"

Seconds ticked by before Densel nodded. "Permission granted." He stepped aside and let the lieutenant cross the threshold into the Command Escape Pod. He turned and said, "Follow us, lieutenant."

Piper smiled and happily followed the others up the ladder to the Living Area. He found a spot at the round table and smelled Grog. "Any for me?"

Densel slowly sat back at his place and said, "Answers first."

"Okay." The young man slowly said. "Sure, anything."

"The box."

Piper had placed the stone box in front of him. "Yes?"

Densel asked, "One, why? Two, what is in it?"

Piper remained silent.

"I have a mind to put you back in your pod . . . it's in the way, mister."

"Sir, the box is the reason we'll be rescued early."

Gordon said, "Come again? That thing?"

Piper nodded, "It's the artifact the Skipper had me announce in the Mayday."

"What's inside?" Steward asked.

Piper placed his hand on top of the box. "Artifacts."

"Open it!" Some said from the back.

Densel noticed Piper didn't flinch. His hand rested firmly on the box.

"It's locked." Piper said emotionless.

Seconds ticked by.

Densel cleared his throat. "Do you know what is inside?"

"Artifacts."

"Like knives, dolls, chipped stone, a comm device? Give lieutenant."

"Artifacts." He repeated.

"Open it."

"I can't."

Densel didn't buy it. "Open it."

Piper swallowed hard. "I don't know the codes."

"So how'd you know to get it? The Old Man never said anything to me about this. . ." he pointed a finger at it, ". . . this box. Even just before abandoning ship he said nothing."

Piper shrugged. "The Skipper had his reasons . . ."

"Bullshit. The Captain never kept secrets from me. I've known him for over fifteen years."

"That can't be helped, but the Skipper is not beholden to you to tell his secrets."

"I married his only daughter!"

Piper paused for a moment. He hadn't thought about that. "Commander. I don't know the codes," and he slide the box toward Densel, "but, I know we should not open it."

"Have you seen the contents?"

He hesitated too long. "Some, not all." He lied.

"And?"

Piper sighed, "Ummm."

"Lieutenant. What am I going to tell ComProp? They're going to come to me first. Do I tell them that Captain Rogers had an alternate agenda? 'Sorry, sirs. But Captain Rogers told me shit about a box that would change the way humans view the entire universe. The most important find in all of human kind is in a stone box I had no knowledge of until after the McCain exploded.' Come on, Piper. "

"The Skipper . . . had his reasons. I just know . . ."

"Lieutenant. We're going to be out here for a very long time."

"Commander, I can't. I promised the Skipper."

"He's dead now."

Piper took a deep breath and exhaled slowly. "Photos and stone tiles with indecipherable writing, and . . ."

"Photos!" Densel exclaimed.

Piper looked down. "Yeah, just simple photos. Of a female . . . we think."

Gordon said, "How can you say 'simple' photos. We know what they look like!"

Piper remained silent.

Steward said, "Dude! This is history and you're downplaying the whole thing. What's up?"

Densel cocked his head toward Piper. "Mister, something is not right here."

Piper remained silent.

"Lieutenant. Within ten minutes we're questioning you. What do you think ComProp is gonna give you?"

Piper looked up.

"It's not fitting. Your reactions, gestures, answers, are all hinky. Think about that."

Piper did. He sighed heavily, reached for the box and tapped in the code for each Security C-Clamp. Each snapped open. He carefully moved the clamps out of the way and gently lifted the lid.

Densel, Gordon, Steward and the others moved in close to peer inside the box.

Gordon said, "That's it?" She reached in to grab a small stone tile.

Piper's hand reached out to stop her but Densel stopped him.

Gordon reached in and pulled out a small translucent metal plate. It had the image of a humanoid woman on it embedded in the center. She looked it over several times. "Impressive, but total fake. And this thing?" She put the picture back and pulled out a wand. "This is supposed to be a magic wand?" She pointed it at Piper.

He flinched and moved her hand away. "That actually works."

Gordon said, "Seriously? All this stuff is fake."

Someone in the back said, "Fake? Seriously?"

"What? This wand is magic?"

Piper shook his head. "It's a Laser."

"Piper!" Gordon said. "Why in the galaxy would anyone think these things real?"

Piper said, "We aged everything."

Densel asked, "How?"

"We age-dated the items using several different techniques. An Absolute Dating analysis sets everything to about 1,000 years ago."

Gordon snouted. "That may be so, but the image is fake. Come on. Couldn't you use an original image? Like create your own 3D model?"

Piper's mind raced. They hadn't really worked out the details. Everything in the box were prototypes and proof of concepts. They would have had another three years to work out the details and tweak the artifacts. "It's not what you think?"

Densel frowned. "Not what we think? You were gonna pawn off some junk to ComProp!"

"Of course not! The pics were experimental. The stone tiles were important . . ."

Steward exclaimed, "And I can't believe the Captain was in on this!"

"He wasn't," Piper said after a sigh. "He found out maybe a month before the emergency. We told him . . ."

Densel interrupted, "We . . . ?"

Piper inhaled and whispered into himself, 'fuck.'

"Well? We?"

"It started out as a joke. You know. Three years to get here and plenty of time for hobbies . . ."

"Go on."

"A few of us sat around one cycle and joked about finding a box of old junk and how ComProp would go ape-shit on how great of a discovery it was."

"Who were the others?" Densel asked.

"I'd rather not say."

"I think you should say, Lieutenant. ComProp doesn't take kindly to fraud."

"It was joke. We seriously had no intention of pushing this off on anyone. We just wanted to see how far we could push the envelope."

"How did the Old Man find out?"

"Remember that surprise Dog watch inspection?"

Densel nodded.

"He walked in on one of the guys working the Electronic Scope. It was the picture. We figured if we could measure isotopes in objects why couldn't we add isotopes. Make it seem a lot younger than what it really is. Or, remove isotopes . . ."

Steward finished, ". . . to make it seem older."

Piper nodded. "The Skipper had mixed feelings. He told Bli . . . the other person to 'carry-on' but send him regular reports on progress."

Densel shook his head. "I had the conn during that watch. He came back in a good mood. Damn! I never saw this coming."

"No one saw it coming. We had no specific aim. We never discussed officially presenting our results. We just did what people do when they are bored stupid – for years. I should have left the box on the ship."

Gordon said, "Why didn't you?"

"Because it's my box. Look, we wouldn't be having this talk if the Skipper hadn't sent that Mayday. And I kind of freaked. So, I went to get it." Piper shook his head slowly and shrugged, "I have issues. I should have left the damn thing on the ship."

Densel nodded, "but you didn't."

The two stared at one another.

Piper blinked first and looked away. "I kept this thing because I didn't want to lose it. We . . . I spent pretty much of three years working out the details. I didn't do it to trick everyone, but to show I could do it."

"There's an 'and' in there."

Piper nodded. He looked around and noticed everyone staring at him. "And, by the off chance someone 'discovered' some of the items years from now and it got them to probe further then that would be . . ." He paused and took a deep breath. "You know, kind of exciting. Of course, I would hope to be on my deathbed when that happened."

Steward said, "Wait, what? You planned on leaving that box on the planet?"

Piper nodded, "Leaning toward that. Twenty, forty, eighty, maybe hundreds of years from now some exo-archaeologist would stumble upon the box and try to uncover its secrets." He started laughing but cut it off short when no one else joined him.

Gordon said, "Sick. Just sick."

Piper scrunched his face up. "I never actually said I was going to do it. It was a thought."

"The Captain sent out a Mayday with false information. ComProp is not going to look kindly on wasting several trillion dollars for a hoax."

Piper sat quietly staring at the box. "It wasn't supposed to happen like this. The Skipper had no reason to lie. It just so happens I have a box that was made to look old." He softly said.

They felt a bump.

The room went silent.

"Another one?" Densel said. He tapped at the table's surface interface. It read, 'Engineering Pod'.

Chapter 3

Piper said, "Computer, pause scene."
Everyone froze in place.
"Wen."
"Yes, Wayne?"
"I don't remember any of this. How accurate is this recreation?"
"Rounded down, it is 92% accurate."
Piper shook his head for several seconds and then ran a hand through his hair. He covered his face with the other hand. "I. Am. Absolutely. Embarrassed."
"Yes, Wayne."
"I'm also mad as hell."
Wen answered, "Because everyone knew what happened and didn't tell you a single thing?"

"That, too." Then after a moment, "Computer, resume scene."

***

Bliff was waiting behind the airlock door to the Command Escape Pod. Behind him was Murphy, the only person he pretty much trusted. Each had a gun. Everyone else was placed in the Stasis pods. He peered through the airlock portal, smiling.

Densel tapped out the open code and stepped back. It took about 30 seconds for the system to complete the cycle. The door hissed open and he felt the bullet hit him in the shoulder before he heard the bang. He stumbled back a bit and collapsed onto the floor. Blood splatter had spotted the wall behind him.

Bliff saw that the first office was down. He aimed the pistol between Densel's eyes and squeezed the trigger.

The gun barked. The bullet struck target.

Densel felt pressure between his eyes . . . then . . .

Bliff and Murphy pointed their guns at a now growing gathering.

Gordon stepped up, "What the fuck! What is wrong with you?!"

"Shut up!" He yelled. "I'm taking over!"

Steward stepped up, "The hell you . . ."

Murphy's gun barked.

Steward dropped where he stood. Bullet in his abdomen. Carolina rushed to his side and put pressure on the wound.

Bliff said, "Any questions?" He looked around. "Well!" He yelled. "Good. I still got enough ammo to answer as many questions asked."

Gordon gave him a hard stare.

Bliff walked over to her. "Glad you made it, love." He unconsciously licked his lips and smiled.

Gordon sneered and took a step back.

"Oh, don't do that doll." His gaze moved from her feet to the top of her head. "We're going to have quality time alright."

She spat at his feet, but said nothing.

Bliff look at his feet for a moment. "I just polished these." He walked over to Gordon. She was visibly scared but stood her ground. "That wasn't nice." He rubbed his foot on the back of her pants leg. "Do that again and I'll use your ass to clean my shoe." He leaned in and kissed her on the forehead.

Gordon flinched to Bliff's satisfaction.

Bliff stepped back a few feet. "Where's the medic?"

Silence.

"Well?"

Carolina said, "All dead. Hull breach."

"Seriously?"

Carolina nodded.

Bliff took deep breath. "Step away from him."

"What?"

"Step away, now."

Carolina hesitated.

Bliff aimed the pistol at Steward's heart and squeezed off a round. He then squeezed another round at Carolina's heart. Blood back splattered the distance to his arm. He turned to Gordon. "Any thoughts?"

She locked eyes with him for a few seconds and looked away.

Bliff scanned the room. Nine were left and he needed to get most of them in stasis or dumped into space. He spotted McDonald off to the right, behind Piper. "Piper! You made it! You bring the box?"

Piper nodded. "Yeah, I did."

"Didja open it?"

Piper held his breath and slowly nodded.

"Pity. Where is it?"

"In the Living section."

Bliff said, "McDonald, you out rank me by a month?"

McDonald stepped away from behind Piper.

Bliff's pistol barked and McDonald crumpled to the deck.

Gordon snapped, "What the fuck! Why are you doing this?"

"Maintaining my dominance of the Command Escape Pod. It's a good thing I promoted before you, right?" One eyebrow lifted up. "Murph, it's time."

Murphy nodded and said, "Everyone to the Stasis Pods."

A few hesitated.

"Stasis pods or a bullet. Easy choice to me."

Within minutes everyone had been placed in stasis except for Gordon and Piper.

Bliff sat in the command chair with Gordon a few chairs over to the left, Murphy a few chairs over on the other right, and Piper standing by the airlock door looking apprehensive. He tapped the command pad and cleared his throat. "All hands, all hands. This is Lieutenant Commander Kingslayer. Commander Densel had an accident and all Medical Staff has been lost due to hull breach in the Medical Escape

Pod. As such, I am in charge. We don't know how long ComProp will take, but it will be at least three years before a rescue team reaches us. Those in individual and squad pods should rig for stasis immediately. The main computer will guide your pod to close proximity to the Med Escape Pod.

Those in Personnel pods should begin emergency rations and stasis rotation until rescue. Start fireguard shifts with the highest ranking person in charge of scheduling. That is all. May the Most High have mercy on our souls." He tapped out the 'off' communicate command and instructed the computer to send the Security Pods toward the planet's surface. He then sent out a system wide command to the other Pods to cluster around the command and medical pods. A few more taps and he shifted the command pod, with the Medical Pod in tow, to a higher orbit. He accessed the computers root function and instructed it to stop recording and delete all video and audio. He tapped out the command for the computer to randomly instruct some of the other Pods to delete video and audio, as well. He looked up and over to Gordon. He decided he loved looking at her mouth and full lips. He imagined she was sucking on a very large straw. A most satisfying imagine, indeed. Then he turned to look at Piper. He, too, had a very pretty mouth he decided. Three years was going to be hell on both of them and that brought a smile to his face.

***

Piper yelled, "Computer, pause scene!" He got up and paced a small area for several minutes. He firmly rapped himself on the forehead a half dozen times. "Why can't I remember any of this?!?"

Wen said, "The Rescue Examiner reported you had several very powerful drugs in your system. Your alcohol blood count was at 2.2. Add all that to the Stasis field and you suffered brain tissue damage."

"But I remember my childhood, the academy."

"But not your time on the McCain. A little more than three years of your life wiped out. The Examiner said you were lucky. There were some individuals under a normal Stasis field lost more than you did. Some permanently impaired."

Piper walked over to a frozen image of Bliff. He yelled, "Fucking bastard! You were my friend! I trusted you . . . you . . . you fuck! How could you?!?" He exhaled.

Wen said, "Feel better?"

"No, I don't. I'm thinking I'm either being played or going through some forced therapy."

"The latter. And it makes sense . . ."

". . . how so?"

"If you knew all this twenty years how do you think it would have affected you?"

Piper frowned.

"Wayne, there is more. And it is not good. "

"Computer," Piper started, "resume scene."

***

"Get me some Grog." Bliff told Gordon.

She remained seated and gave him a hard stare.

Bliff got up, walked to her chair, and stopped within striking distance. "Get me some Grog!"

Gordon's body started to tremble. "It's over in the Kitchen section marked 'Grog', you can't miss it." She tried to make the words come out strong.

Bliff gave her a fast strike to the face.

Piper said, "Bliff, I'll get it for you."

"No, I want Ms. Admiral's daughter to get it."

"But Bliff . . ." Piper started.

"Is going to get me Grog!"

Visibly shaken Gordon said, "No. Shoot me then."

Bliff roared in anger, grabbed her by the back of her head and violently shoved her to her knees. He bent down getting very close to her face. "I was hoping you would say no. Piper knows what's in store for him. You, miss bitch . . . you are expendable. No one to help you. No one to save you. No one awake who would give a fuck about what's gonna happen to you."

Dread and terror seemed to press against her heart. Gordon hoped she'd piss him off hard enough that he'd shot her from impulse. Imagining years in space with this bully was terrifying.

"I'd be happy enough to fuck your dead body until it started to stiffen. With you, makes no difference. You are trillions of kilometers from anyone thinking about your doomed ass." He let go of her hair.

She saw that Bliff was getting hard, which meant one end for her. Nodding, she got up and walked into the Kitchen area. Her father told her that every Pod had a secret compartment with hard alcohol.

Only Command Deck officers knew how to access it. She slid her hand along the underside of the main counter and found the button. She pushed it and a small panel slid open just over the sink. She reached in and felt several padded cylinders. She pulled out one and read the markings. "Spiced Rum, Oakheart, Bacardi, 2165." The cylinder was about 30 centimeters tall and 12 in diameter. She popped the safety seal and unscrewed the cap. A sweet aroma filled the air. She took out four plastic cups from a nearby cabinet and filled each one up. She recapped the rum and took the cups to the Living Area Section. Bliff seemed disappointed that she hadn't fought further and harder, but he smiled when the first wisps of Spiced Rum reached his nostrils.

Murphy slipped out of his seat and hurried over to Bliff and Gordon. "Is that what I think it is?"

Gordon nodded.

"The real shit?"

She nodded again.

Piper started to get out of his seat when Murphy pointed the pistol at his head. "The seat for you, Piper. She'll bring it to you."

Piper swallowed hard, nodded, and sat back down.

Bliff asked, "How many?"

"Two more left, maybe a third. Hard to tell. Don't know what they are."

"Your Daddy tell you this?"

Gordon frowned. She wasn't sure if Bliff was working his way to insulting her or teasing.

He smiled, "Any other secrets?"

She shook her head knowing full well there were other secrets. Like several unlocked guns fully loaded. Or that several carbine knives were also hidden.

Bliff took a cup and handed it to Murphy. He took a second cup for himself and nodded to Gordon.

She walked over to Piper.

He reached out, "Thank you," and took a cup with trembling hands. Some of the liquor spilled onto the floor. He steadied his hand with the other one and took a long sip. The Rum burned and he nearly coughed.

Bliff took a swig. He relaxed and took off his boots. "Get comfortable. We're gonna be here a while."

Gordon held her cup up to her lips and sipped. She didn't think she'd make it to one of the secret spots fast enough. Two were on the

Command deck, with the third in the Living area. She took a second sip when she realized Bliff had been undressing her with his eyes.

"Get comfortable, Gordon. I insist."

She took off her boots.

"More. And, slowly please."

"Fuck you!" She spat.

"I was hoping you'd give me some attitude." He answered.

"Shoot me, you Bastard!"

Bliff smiled. "I have a better idea." He rushed over and grabbed her by the arm. He took her to the ladder and shoved her at the ladder. "Get down there!"

She hesitated for a moment and the butt of the pistol connected to the side of her head. She nearly blacked out, but the back of his hand to her face was enough to wake her up.

"Get down there now!" He shouted. "I can do worse than shoot you in the head."

She started down the ladder only to be kicked in the head. When she stepped away Bliff was close.

He pushed her to one of the Stasis beds. "I'm guessing you aren't the selfish bitch you act like and you like some of these people."

She said nothing.

"I'm also guessing that you don't want to feel guilty for me shooting one of them in the head. Am I right?"

She stared at the container. Molly was still. Her red hair was loose and flowed across either side of the pillow.

Bliff punched in the latch release.

The Stasis container cycled through the unlock sequence and started the process on reviving Molly.

Bliff lifted up the lid. "After I had finished with you I was gonna let you sleep and wake up Molly here. But I changed my mind."

Gordon jumped as Bliff's pistol barked. She was back splattered with Molly's brain and blood.

Bliff leaned in close to her ear and whispered, "Eight more to go here. After that I'll bring in some of the smaller personnel pods and start this all over again. We are alone. Daddy ain't gonna be flying in to rescue his little girl anytime soon. This is day one." He lowered his voice further. She could barely hear him. "I have nothing to lose. I've crossed the line and no one can stop me." He backed away.

Gordon's eyes teared up. Grief and doom clenched at her heart hard. "You bastard," she whispered.

Bliff smiled. "Wash up and meet me upstairs. Take too long I'll come down and shoot someone else." He turned and walked off leaving Gordon shaken.

She tightly hugged herself and thought of the hidden guns. Then she thought of Murphy. At some point one or both would have to sleep. Could she pull the trigger? She walked over to one of the personal shower units and set the water to hot. She scrubbed herself hard for ten minutes trying to rid the feel of Molly's remains on her face. After drying off she decided to stay naked. Bliff would just have to accept that. As she climbed up the ladder she could hear Piper's muffled screams. Bliff was working him from behind while Murphy made him suck. Piper struggle but had his arms held behind him by Bliff.

Gordon could see that Murphy's member was small with an enlarged mushroom like tip. The rumors had been true and Murphy usually had to pay crew for sex. Bliff, on the other hand, was large. Several of the females called it "The Meat" and only said 'Once was enough'. Some of the males voiced the same opinion, thus Bliff had a short list of willing participates. Typically, he bullied for sex and only a blowjob at that. Scuttle had it that his last intercourse encounter was over a year ago and that person had been hospitalized for a torn sphincter.

Bliff growled as he pumped harder and longer. "Almost there."

Murphy started shaking and his hips worked frantically against Piper's face. A few seconds later Murphy fell back. "Fuck that was great."

Piper continued to scream and Bliff yelled, "Shut up. I'm almost there."

Gordon was fixated on this rape scene. She was horrified, afraid, and guiltily aroused.

Bliff punched Piper several times in the back of the head to make him stop screaming. He liked the screams but he needed to concentrate now and Piper just wouldn't shut up. With a dozen more powerful long strokes he felt the familiar tingling sensation and gave one last hard stroke just before he came. A dozen pulsating spasms left him weak and gasping for breath. He collapsed on top of an unconscious Piper and nuzzled the back of his head. He pulled out and walked over to the sink. He took a cloth and soaked it with warm water. Then he wiped off Piper's blood, smiling as he felt the warmth on the cloth. He knew Gordon was going to feel just as good. "I'm good for a while." He said smiling at her.

She walked to Piper and felt for a pulse. It was faint but there. She went over to one of the side cabinets and pulled out a Med-Kit. She opened it and found the items she needed.

Piper regained consciousness as Gordon knelt down beside him. She gave him a fast acting painkiller and a small carton of STIM juice.

She rolled him over and applied ointment.

He winced. Not quite embarrassed that she was fingering his ass with medication, but that he liked her fingering his ass.

She placed a cold pack to his anus after she finished. After closing the case she walked over to the sink. She left the case on the counter and washed her hands in hot water. She figured it was only a matter of time before she needed medication.

Murphy watched with going arousal. He went both ways and thought a mouth was good for eating, sucking, and swallowing – regardless of the gender.

Gordon walked over to Piper and started wiping him clean of blood and semen with anti-bacterium wipes from the Med-kit.

He lifted himself up to her and whispered. "I can't imagine three or more years of this."

She nodded, got up and disposed of the wipes in the recycler. She went back and collected the remaining plastic cups and refilled them with Spiced Rum. She checked in the cooler and found cherry flavored water. She topped four cups with it and passed them out.

***

"Computer, pause scene."

"Wayne, are you okay?"

Tears streamed down his cheeks. "They raped me. I can't believe it. I was . . . raped . . . by. That. Bastard!" He jabbed a finger hard at Bliff's image." He wiped the tears from his cheeks. "I don't know what I would have done twenty years ago if they told me." Taking a deep breath he said, "Computer, resume scene."

***

Bliff said, "Now this is more like it. What are you going to cook?"

Gordon grimaced for a moment and then smiled. "Checking." She found the stash of freeze-dried goods and pulled several out. Her favorite was beef stew. She figured Bliff liked meat and potatoes and cheese. She found two packs within arm's reach and placed them on the counter. Murphy she would give Puerto Rican rice and pork strips. Piper needed liquids, at least for a week or more. She found the freeze-dried ice cream and decided he needed chocolate and vanilla swirl. After several minutes she had everything reconstituted with hot water. For herself she opted for chicken noodle soup. She pulled out several flat trays and placed the packages on the trays. She had filled each package with the appropriate amount of water. Then she thought of the guns. One was hidden nearby. She scanned the counter and found the tall-tale sign of the secret spot. It was easy to make out the release button once she knew what to look for. All too easy. 'Yes,' she thought. 'I would pull the trigger. Several times and then some.' She turned, nearly bumping into Bliff.

He smirked and nuzzled the side of her head. "You smell nice."

The reflex to gag was almost tripped, but she swallowed hard and took a deep breath. She choked out, "Thanks."

"Seriously, you smell nice. I like that."

Gordon could tell Bliff was about ready for another round, but with her this time. She uttered, "Food."

He looked down and nodded. "Yeah, food first, then feast." He laughed to himself as he took a seat at the table.

Murphy took a spot opposite Bliff. His small member stiff and jutting out.

Gordon looked at it. The sight would have been comical if not for their present predicament. She placed the trays in front of Bliff and Murphy. She was mindful to pour more Rum into their cups.

Bliff and Murphy ate ravenously. Together, they consumed another four packages of food and half the Rum. Gordon thought either they were really that hungry, or they wanted to get the distraction of nourishment out of the way to take care of something more important.

Murphy leaned back and belched. He upended the cup and held it out. "Not bad for processed food."

Gordon walked over, poured him another cup and collected the empty cartons and containers.

Murphy slapped her ass hard. He laughed as he watched a red hand shaped spot on one of her cheeks darken.

Bliff got up and stretched. He decided he finally had to use the bathroom. "Murph, I'm going to the head. Watch them for me?"

He nodded and took another swig from the cup. His eyes had a glassy sheen to them and the eyelids were about half way closed. He stood up and nearly fell.

Both men laughed.

Gordon noted that neither guarded their weapons closely.

Bliff picked up on that. He smiled, grabbed the gun and tossed it toward Gordon.

She nearly dropped it, but caught it looking puzzled.

"Darlin', that gun is coded for Murph and myself."

She wrapped her fingers around the handle.

He nodded, "That's it, sweet cheeks. Feel that grip. I want you to hold my cock like that when it is in your mouth."

Gordon's expression turned dark. She aimed the pistol at Bliff's head.

"You know, I gotta take a dump, so I'm in a hurry. Pull the trigger or put it down."

She remembered what they did to Piper and squeezed the trigger.

Both she and Bliff jumped when the hammer clicked loudly.

He smiled and said, "Now you know."

Gordon's shoulders slumped. Panic was setting in and she was next. They've been fed, are now drunk, and soon it would be her turn. She reached over to the space of hidden alcohol after pressing the button and pulled out another container. This one was marked 'Champagne'.

"What are you doing over there?!?" Murphy shouted.

"Getting us something special . . ." She pressed the release button for a hidden carbine.

Murphy started walking toward her.

Gordon turned around to show him the container. "See. I think I need something different than rum."

"What is it?" Murphy slurred.

"Champagne."

His expression lightened. "Champagne. Been a long time." He moved back to the table and toyed with his gun. He was thinking that maybe Bliff wouldn't mind if he started on Gordon first, like he had with Piper. But then he was a little too drunk to really start anything. He finished the cup of Rum and liked his lips. Should he have Champagne or sleep? He chuckled to himself. He could sleep when he was dead he thought. He and Bliff had nothing to worry about. They talked about this for some time and things were going well. 'Man,' he thought. Gordon was probably sweet tasting. He put the cup down to see Gordon slice a carbine sideways in front him. He thought that she looked lovely when she was angry, before he felt a sharp pain. He couldn't get a good breath and felt something wet go down his throat. He noted Gordon was suddenly covered in blood. She cut his throat. He was going to die. The bitch cut his throat and he was going to die. Drunk, naked, and mutilated. He was going to die. Fuck he thought. Then he felt a sharp pain in his chest. 'The bitch pierced my heart' he thought.

Bliff stepped off the ladder. He smelled blood before he realized what it was. Murphy was slumped over a pool of blood. He saw Piper and Gordon off to one side.

"Stupid, Cunt!" He yelled out. He looked around and spotted his gun still on the counter. He ran over and picked it up. It felt lighter than he remembered but he aimed it at her.

Gordon moved her other hand from around her body to show she had a gun, too.

Bliff laughed. "That's Murphy's gun. It won't work for you." He squeezed the trigger.

The click was deafening.

Bliff squeezed the trigger several more times, then he looked up.

Gordon tossed the rounds from the magazine onto the floor. "Stupid, fuck!" And she pulled the trigger.

Bliff felt the round strike his abdomen as he heard the gun bark. He thought, 'damn, but it was good a run' and looked over to Gordon as he collapsed to the floor. He could smell her now musky scent. His one regret would be to not have raped her. He should have shot her instead of Molly.

Gordon stood over Bliff now. She spat at his face and said, "Fucker. I hate you." Three more rounds to the head prevented Bliff from answering.

***

The holoscene ended.

"I knew it! Wendy saved us."

Wen said, "Yes, Wayne. She did. Sub-consciously you've been carrying that feeling all this time."

Piper nodded. "Wen?"

"Yes, Wayne?"

"How do you feel about that?"

"Lieutenant Commander Gordon committing murder?"

Piper rubbed his chin and frowned. "I hadn't thought of it that way. I was a victim, which is still sickening to think about. She stepped up and saved both of us."

"How do you feel not being the rescuer?"

"Embarrassed. I didn't fight hard enough, I . . ."

"Would have been killed if you had . . ."

"Maybe . . ."

Wen interrupted, "No maybe. It would have happened."

"Okay, okay, but you haven't answered my question yet."

"Wayne, I am a Synthetic Intelligence. I don't really 'feel'. I cannot 'feel'."

"Wen, bullshit. You 'feel' no less than I do."

"We've had this discussion before and . . ."

". . . I end up not buying a single word. We have been down this road before. Agree to disagree. For now."

Wen answered, "Agreed to disagree. But the Holoscenes?"

"Computer, resume scene."

The computer said, "That is the end, Commander."

Piper said, "Seriously? That's it? Wen?"

Wen said, "Checking."

After a few moments Wen said, "Wayne, the encrypted file is the next scene."

Piper swallowed hard. A lump seemed to have formed in the center of his throat. "I'm not going to like this. I think I know the passcode."

Wen said, "That was it. Are you ready?"

"You've seen it?"

Wen remained silent.

"Wen? You've seen it?"

"I have."

"And?"

"Maybe I do 'feel'."

"Wen?"

"Yes."

"What did I do?"

The silence lasted thirty seconds.

Piper repeated. "What did I do?"

The scene started.

***

Piper walked up to Gordon and slowly pulled the gun from her hands. She looked over to Piper and said, "I'm tired."

He nodded and led her to the table.

Murphy's corpse was in the way and the two had to step over it. The Pod's cleaner bots started working. There were half way done absorbing the blood on the floor when Piper walked back to the kitchen area and retrieved the container of Champagne. He placed the gun on the counter and walked back to the table. He handed Gordon the container.

She took it and drank deeply. "Fuck! That tasted good." She said breathless. She passed the container to Piper.

He took it and drank just as deeply. He wiped his lips and burped loudly.

Both smiled and laughed.

Piper got up and said, "I really don't want to clean this mess up now."

Gordon nodded. "The bots are doing a good job. We'll have to put the fuckers somewhere."

"The same pod that the Commander and Steward are in."

She started to tear up and nodded. "We'll have to get the Security Pods docked and . . ."

Piper interrupted, "I can do that. Get some rest. If Bliff locked out the computer we can wait for you to unlock it."

Gordon hesitated.

"It's not like we're in any danger now. Besides, I can check all CommPacks. Remember, it's what I do."

She nodded and smiled slightly. "I'll shower and sleep in one of the Sleep units. Goddess knows I want to sleep in a bed and not a chair."

Piper nodded. "Wake you up in a few hours?"

"Please."

A moment later she was gone. Piper found his pair of pants and shirt and put them on. He climbed up to the Command deck and sat in the Command chair. After tapping through a few options he was relieved that Bliff had not locked the computer. He felt a sense of guilt when he discovered Bliff had sent the Security Pods to the surface of the planet. With luck they all survived intact. A few more taps at the screen revealed that three of the four pods made it safely, but there was no way they would be getting back to space. It would be another eight hours before he could communicate with the surviving pods due to the planet's rotation.

Another check revealed that there were about a couple of dozen empty single personnel pods. That was good news. He instructed the computer to dock two of them with the Command Pod. His mind raced. Bliff had been the mastermind to the would-be hoax, but would ComProp buy it? He got up and walked down into the Living area. The first thing he saw was blood in one of the Units. He walked passed it and found Gordon soundly sleeping. She looked absolutely beautiful he thought. With a heavy heart he closed the Unit's lid and locked it. He then started the Stasis cycle and set it to six months. Now he was alone. The weight of grief washed over him - he was about to cross the line. After verifying that Gordon entered Stasis he made his way back up to the Living Area and entered the Medical Pod through the connecting airlocks.

It was easy to navigate through the Pod. Essentially, it was Medical, and only during an emergency would the entire section turn into an Escape Pod. After a moment he found the pharmacy and rifled through the cabinets. The drugs he was looking for were clearly marked as "dangerous" – Propranolol, Ethandiazepoxide, and Hydrocodone. He took two tablets from each bottle, found some latex gloves, returned to the Command Escape Pod. He slipped on the gloves and dragged Bliff and Murphy to the Storage area. Piper had to drop them down the ladder shaft, which made his stomach queasy. Both landed hard with a wet smack and Bliff's corpse broke its back with a loud sickening crack. He then climbed down the ladder and dragged both bodies to one of the airlocks. Bliff's body was impossibly twisted and made Piper's stomach protest. He swallowed hard and made the climb to the Command Deck quick. He checked on the progress of the two pods. The readings said another three hours. So, Piper went down to the Living area and made himself a meal – Beef Stroganoff with red wine sauce, mashed potatoes and gravy, gouda cheese and water crest crackers. The drink was Tang and dessert was Key lime crème bulee. He took his time and slowly chewed. The box was next to him, untouched. The box. The one with the artifacts. The one that could possibly get him jailed or in a best scenario kicked out of Fleet if ComProp didn't buy any of his story. He took another drink from the container of champagne. And then in the midst of wandering thoughts he felt a bump. He climbed down the ladder to the Storage area and peeked out the airlock. A Pod was docked. Several seconds later the other Pod docked. Piper took a deep breath and tapped out the open sequel on one of the airlocks.

Thirty seconds later the door hissed opened. He grabbed Bliff by the leg and dragged him into the Pod. Murphy was lighter so it was easy to toss him on top of Bliff. He closed the door and tapped out the close sequence. Piper pondered for a moment, sighed, then made his way to the Command Deck. He sat in the Command chair and tapped out the detach sequence for the two Pods. The course he set in was a high orbit that would eventually aim the Pod to drop orbit and smash into the planet. He did the same thing for the Pod with Densel and Steward. Next he went back down into the Kitchen area and sealed the box up. He walked over to the Kitchen area and grabbed the carbine Gordon used earlier. Tears started running down his cheeks as he climbed down the ladder to the Stasis Units. One by one he punctured the kevlar covered oxygen mix line. It took him about twenty minutes of nicking, punching, digging, scratching, piercing each line. The soft hiss of gas told him death for each person was just a matter of time. He entered the lock code for each unit to prevent the system from initiating its rescue mode. Maybe a day, maybe two, each person would die quietly in their dreamless sleep. What was most heartbreaking of all for him was sabotaging Gordon's Unit, but they all had to go. After he finished the last Unit he gathered the rest of his clothes and pushed them down the recycling bin. He found a set of flight jumpers and put one on. Grabbing the container of champagne he filled his mouth and sucked in all six pills. He had twenty minutes before they would take effect. He hurried down the ladder to the Storage area and got into the last Pod. He belted himself in the chair and punched in the codes to detach from the Command Escape Pod. He tapped out an orbit plan that would eventually align his Pod up with the ones out along the fringe parameter.

His eyesight started to blur and concentrating was becoming difficult. He pressed the start button and the Pod detached. Once it started its ascent he tapped out the Start Stasis process. The drugs were starting to take effect now. He was gripped with euphoria and had a hard time remembering what he was doing in the Pod. It was something about an emergency, maybe. Piper looked out one of the Pod windows. He could see a large cluster of Pods surrounding three larger Pods. One Pod had a large tear across the top. Something bad must have happened. 'Sucks to be us', he thought just before he blacked out.

Chapter 4

Piper said out loud, "I'm a murderer. A selfish, immature murderer." He stood up for a moment only to have his legs buckle. The landing was hard but Piper welcomed it. "Wen, I am a murderer. And they knew it! Every single goddamn Admiral, Examiner, Council member knew it."

"Wayne, you are not the person 60 years ago."

"How can you say that?!? I killed Wendy!"

Wen slowly said, "Yes, you killed Lieutenant Commander Gordon sixty years ago, but the person you were then is not the same person now. You suffered brain tissue damage to the point that effectively you are different."

Piper shook his head vigorously for a few seconds.

"Wayne, you went through an extensive vetting. GRID Central would have never let you resume service if they thought you were unworthy . . ."

"But . . ."

"No buts, that's the way of GRID and The Most High. Lieutenant Commander Gordon was a Most High. Her Father the Admiral was a Most High. You were not. Think about that."

Piper ran a hand through his hair. "I'm a Most High now . . . kind of."

"Wayne, forgive, but don't forget."

"How can you say that?"

"I can never forget, but I can forgive."

Piper frowned. "But you're a . . ."

"Synthetic Intelligent, yes. And, you were right. I do feel. I just don't like to advertise it."

"Wen . . ." Piper paused and couldn't decide what he wanted to say.

"Fundamentally, you are a different person."

"How so?"

"You suffered brain tissue damage. Psyche scans verify you have little to no recognition to what happened 20 years ago. Therefore, you are different."

"I don't think I can forgive myself – yet."

Wen replied, "It's a start."

"Agreed." Admiral Ty said from the back of the room.

Piper jumped when he heard his Boss' voice. "Admiral! Not expected!'

Ty smiled. "I never am."

Piper said, "How much of this did you know?"

"Up until six months ago, very little." He shrugged. "Only what was in the official reports. The Holoscenes are property of The Most High."

Piper said, "Wen?"

"The Admiral is telling the truth."

Ty, surprised, said, "Wayne? I've withheld info from you, but never lied."

Piper laughed. "Which is usually seen as the same thing."

Ty nodded. "Point, but, seriously. I trust you. You've saved my life once and how can I forget that?"

Piper took a deep breath. "I'm a goddamn murderer!"

"Sixty years ago and that you is technically gone." Ty replied.

"Technically?!? I'm the same person."

Ty shook his head slowly. "The Examiner's report says you suffered enough brain tissue damage to have altered your personality. Forty years in stasis was the best thing for you."

"Murder is still murder."

The room went silent for several moments.

Ty finally said, "You have two choices."

"They are?"

"Live or suicide. I don't have a lot of time."

Piper felt the weight of his words. Would he be able to live out his life in peace knowing what he knows now? Would he be able to look into a mirror and stare into eyes of a selfish coward?

"You are of The Most High. You have served GRID selflessly. You have followed in the footsteps of giants whose only mission was to solve crimes. You've risked your life to save countless others. I have a folder with hundreds of heroic acts from you. Nearly twenty years of helping people. You've given to the cause and then some. How can I not call you Brother?"

"But . . ." Piper started.

"Wayne, you've been beating yourself up for twenty years."

"What about Wendy?"

"Wen uses Wendy Gordon's voice. You visit her sister every few months and you pay respect to a dozen other crew members' grave sites. You've been subconsciously carrying this burden in your head.

Your night terrors."

"But I'm still a murderer. I should pay for my crimes."

"How many lives have you saved since then?"

Piper shook his head. "Doesn't matter."

Ty grabbed him by the shoulders. "It does matter."

Piper started to protest.

"You've been beating yourself up for twenty years. You became an Investigator to help solve crimes. Now you've solved your own – and you can still solve crimes . . . on your own."

Piper snapped. "It's that easy for you?!?"

Ty let go of his shoulders. "It is." His stare into Piper's eyes were intense. "It is that easy. So, don't forgive yourself." He shrugged. "At least think about what you have and can do. If you want to take your own life no one will stop you."

Piper returned Ty's gaze. Debt paid by suicide? That would be too easy. They have pills to help you cope, he thought. One or two would make you never care about anything or anyone around you. You'd be blissfully happy at being selfish and uncaring. "All that easy?"

Ty replied, "As easy as you want to make it."

"Alright. I'll think about it."

"Good, because I have one more thing for you."

"Wait. This case. There is no case, is there?"

Ty smiled. He liked Wayne. "It was solved ten years ago, but you needed to solve the mystery of your past. And, you did."

Piper frowned. "So, why go through that?"

"She wanted you to go through it."

"She? You mean . . ."

"Erickson."

Piper asked, "Now what?"

With a wide grin, Ty said, "We see The Most High."

Epilogue

The Most High and GRID Central were not going to press forward with charges. They gave him an option: Suicide or Service. It was a hard decision. For twenty years he had been driven to help others and solve crimes. He was good at it too. But this thing. This crime he had done. Had he done all he could do? Piper set his meds on the nightstand and laid down. He decided not to take his meds tonight. He wanted to dream, he needed to dream, he had to dream. And, for the first time in over twenty years, he slept soundly. Burden released, sins acknowledged. Suicide was still an option. That would never be taken off the table, but for now, he could sleep like a normal person for once – bad dreams or not.

###

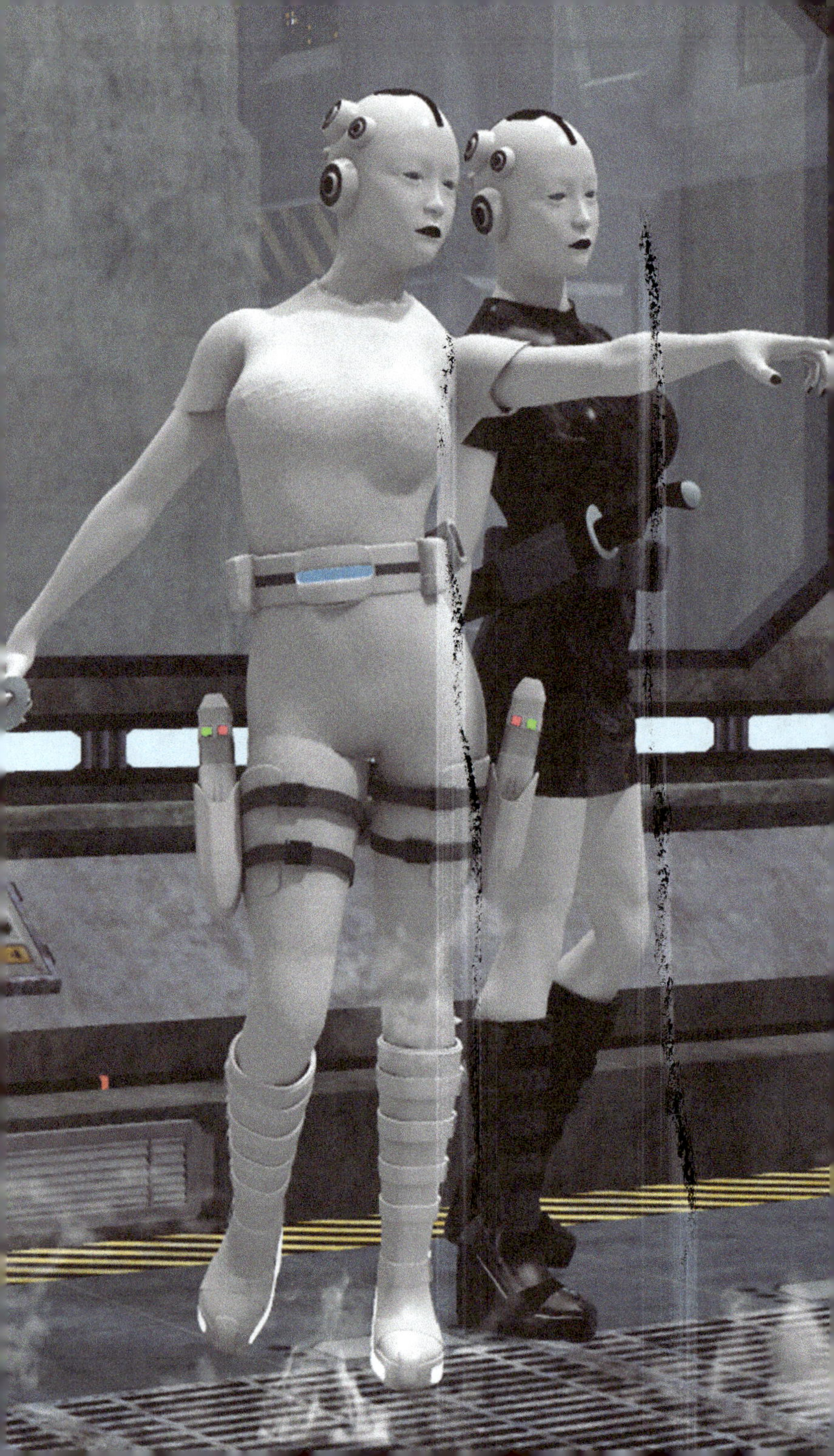

BENEATH RED TAIL WINGS

Part 1
Patricia I. Williams

Prologue

September 1873

The festering strips burned, the fever sucked him dry. The voice of his father harangued his ears, accusing.

"Traitorous, wretched boy! No son of mine would do such a thing!"

"How could you do this? Did you think of us, you bastard? Do you know what this means?"

The echo of the door slamming against his battered jaw pounded on his ears until he cried out.

The Captain would hear. He would come and the beatings would begin again.

"Quiet, quiet boy. You want to get caught? You want to the mate to strike with that devilish belayin' pin? You want to lay in the fo'c'sle waiting to die from another beating? You want to run up and down and up and down for days and nights without sleep or vittles? You want to live boy?"

"No no more, no more. Shut up Papa, shut up. You said follow my conscience. You said be a man and make a stand. I made it Papa. I made it. Ah, don't hate me Papa. Please listen, please!"

"Get out, get out traitorous, wretched boy! Don't show your face again. Traitor!"

He wanted to deny forsaking his family. But the truth could not be denied. They were dead. Father and Royal were dead years gone now, hating him, the traitor. He must keep moving or the Captain would find him. Fearing the tarred ropes and belaying pins striking from the dark, he crawled away from the dock. His body was soaking wet, trembling one moment and burning the next. Desperate, Matthew sucked the briny damp from his filthy shirt. He curled into a stack of cargo already strapped down to be loaded onto another hell ship. He could hear the crowd yelling, demanding the Captain's surrender. He could barely see through his irritated eyes, one swollen shut from a nasty cut and blow to the face he got from a knife or marlinspike. He had never seen it coming.

Charlie had been taken ashore, but the rest of them were not allowed to leave. Lucky Charlie. Say what you want, but he wished he had a friend in this city full of crimps. Benjamin called them that. Crimps. Slave catchers. Need a body? Take it. Matthew was no sailor and tried to explain to the First Mate he was taken under duress. His protest got him a beating. The worst of his life in fact. He had no idea how long he was insensible, but when he was able to stagger from the ragged hammock Harris came and beat him again. Matthew was sure he defended himself the first time, but not this time. There was a belaying pin. He came to, chained to the grates on deck and flogged. It would not be the last time. Mr. Maloney told him to cease resisting and go along so he would stay alive. He was so weak from the beatings and flogging, further protest was impossible anyway.

Months later, Matthew realized it made little difference if he was subservient. He kept his head down and learned to do the work, but feared he would not see land again. Three of the battered crew died. The story was they jumped overboard or fell by accident, but Matthew would always wonder if Harris had outright killed them. Poor John, he was just a boy. Everyone was starving on hardtack and little water. He was shamed he survived because Harris' ire shifted to someone else and they died.

Matthew didn't know if Benjamin put him over the side tonight hoping he would drown or make it out. The man's loyalties shifted each day. There was some talk about a Sailor's Home for help. Matthew didn't know this place and thought it was a fool's errand.

Ben said if he stayed he might just die. He was too weak to fight Ben's insistence. The tide tried to take him away but he grabbed the anchor line and hung on until he got his bearings. The horrific sting of the cold salt water stole his breath. He believed he would drown for sure. How he managed to get onto the pier remained a miracle to him. His nails tore off at the quick from his desperate effort to climb the ladder. The men on the dock were yelling for the Captain's blood, many drunk and angry waving torches and rope for a hanging.

Matthew had enough sense left to scuttle away through stacks of cargo into the shadows between buildings. Rats squealed and ran about in the darkness. He prayed no other crimps found him. Benjamin said if he got caught he would wind up on another ship even broken as he was. Matthew decided he would kill himself for sure to escape another hellish journey like this. His overtaxed body soon failed him. His last thought was he would die in mud reeking of urine and feces.

*****

Birds were singing. He must be lying in the four poster with the balcony doors open to catch an errant breeze. The birds were singing and Matthew's heart reveled in gratitude. For some reason he was especially glad to hear those chirping ditties that used to drive him mad when he wanted to lie in. He was safe now. Somehow all was forgiven and he was home. He waited for his mother to come to him with a cool glass of spring water. Where was she? He was so thirsty.

Father Arturo shook his head in great dismay. Brother Finley worked at his side through the night washing away the filth and cleaning infected wounds across the young man's back and sides. Finley worked with tears in his own eyes until sent away to sleep. In four hours they would trade places beside the cot in the ongoing effort to save this poor soul.

When conscious, the man struggled against the bindings that kept him on his stomach. His back was exposed to the air, the flesh extremely raw from the lancing of the wounds and the harsh carbolic acid wash. The priest hoped he would not be reduced to begging honey or vinegar to keep the wounds clean of further infection. He was grateful a recent graduate of Tolands Medical College had dared to set up practice nearby. The young English doctor was brimming with enthusiasm and new ideas, but had a razor sharp tongue. That was evident when they were all flayed for washing the wounds out with the carbolic, which was supposed to be used to clean the room! Father Arturo feared the realities of life the seamen endured would crush the young man's idealism and fervor.

There was certainly little money to support a practice. The doctor would probably leave for a more prosperous part of town and perhaps do charitable work out of St. Mary's. For now Father Arturo would be grateful to God for His mercy and timely intervention that this life may be saved.

Collapsing onto the stool, Arturo's prayers gave way to the meditative stanzas of the Rosary through which he asked the Blessed Mother to pray for the boy's deliverance. Jesus would surely see to it he roused if the poor soul took a turn for the worse. The exhausted man ignored the racket from the street. The humid air was not very good for a sick soul, heavy with foul odors as it was. But leaving the boy to breath air thick with sick and blood could not be good either. So they left the shutters ajar.

Shouting men carried on with the labor of the day. Harness jangled, horses and mules whinnied and brayed. The high pitched voices of children piped up hawking the home grown vegetables for their mothers. The meager goods were spread out on blankets in the street. The less fortunate children handed out advertising bills from more nefarious employers. Occasionally the sounds would escalate, fueled by arguments and the crack of whips. When the day began to wane, hysterical laughter and screams would add to the chaotic music from the saloons and cribs several blocks away. These dens of iniquity enticed the day laborers to throw away their pitiful earnings on drink and fornication. They were a small part of the overwhelming number that infested the city like fleas.

The priest's efforts to turn men from this folly had not been fruitful. Father Arturo labored against a rising tide of sin from the clapboard structure his group moved into. After driving out the rats and roaches, they offered reasonably clean cots and what medicine they had available from donations. Sometimes medicine was what they stirred up in the kitchen. There were a few men who turned up for confession, weeping over their inability to fight the addiction to liquor and opium. Prayers were said, comfort given and the cycle would begin again. By the Grace of God he escaped many promised beatings from the owner of the local establishments. The sailors and freight drivers threatened to burn the saloon down if hands were laid on a priest or the lay brothers who offered them succor. Sometimes that care was only reasonably clean water and rags to wash away blood, before these men waded back into the cesspit that was their daily life.

Father Arturo dipped the chair back against the gray wall to rest his aching head. Brother Finley woke him up at dawn. The lay brother was upset about resting all night while the priest remained on watch. Arturo listened, mildly amused, to the tirade as he checked on their sleeping patient once more.

The days faded into one another, a sad parade with tired men struggling to save a soul with no desire left to survive. When conscious the poor boy stared as if horror struck for endless hours. His voice was lost completely after screaming, crying and begging through relentless nightmares. Their touch, their very presence finally became unremarked. Exhaustion forced his eyes to shut but when awake, only the stare. The doctor declared his mind was possibly broken forever. But Father Arturo would not give up. They forced broth into the unresisting husk at every opportunity, continued to treat his wounds and prayed.

*****

Four months later Matthew made the effort to stand on his own two legs. He did not know if he was grateful to these men who labored so hard to save him. Two thick limbs from a tree were held in shaky fists propping him up. He remained plagued by bouts of dizziness and his vision seem to be impaired for the long haul. Sometimes the battered muscles in his thighs and legs cramped so tightly he feared they would tear loose from his bones. Dr. Everley assured him that time would resolve these issues, but Matthew worried he was going blind as some days his vision appeared worse than others. Assurances meant nothing to him at this point. He'd been blind before.

His recovery was tedious, the depression worse than any he suffered during the war. Fear was a specter which hovered over his shoulders. What if Harris or the Captain found out he was here and not dead overboard? What if someone carried the tale? He knew from the priest there had been searches carried out. Accusations of bribery, outright lies and speculation had fueled gossip and many outright fights in the street outside their doors. He avoided reading about the searches and the trial of the Sunrise. For the first time in his life Matthew was unsure he could stand up for what was right. The desire to flee was all there was left of him. Even after Father Arturo declared the monstrous duo incarcerated, fear dogged his waking and sleeping hours.

His letter to McNamara had gone unanswered so far. Therein he confided in his law partner about the attack and his subsequent travail at sea. Expressing his desire to be shut of the city and Harris, Matthew wished only to be gone and rebuild his life. The priest had sent an accompanying letter stating how he had found Matthew and the months of recovery. Matthew truly hoped he could be smuggled out of the city without Harris finding out. He was plagued by nightmares of the man. He would awaken choking on bile and gagging and sometimes crying aloud. It shamed him to be in such a state.

Why had he survived the war against his kin and the Indians only to come to this? Was it punishment for taking the stand which betrayed his family and way of life? Was God truly seeing him as a turncoat? Would he ever see his way clear of guilt and punishment? All he had left was a thorough disillusionment with life and the conviction one day he would be even more helpless when the periodic blindness was a permanent state. Even if he could remain in law for now, how could he go before a jury or make a living once blind?

Matthew eased into an old pea coat and made his way out the back door of the derelict storefront. He grimaced at the pull of scar tissue on his back. He wished to forget the horrible experience of the brothers forcing him to move about so the worst of the scars would not cripple him.

The priest and his assistants barely managed to get by in their efforts to minister to the riff raff that populated this area off the waterfront.

Matthew didn't even know where they were in the city. He never asked. What did it matter?

He eased down upon an old crate and let the weak sun attempt to warm his exhausted body. The yard was muddy with only a rope strung between the building and a pole for the endless washing. The ragged bedding stirred in the chill breeze. Matthew realized some of the stains that would not wash away were caused by his own blood. Everything was washed and scrubbed and used again. The brother's hands were raw and calloused from their constant labor and scalding water. No one gave a damn, not about them and not about him. No one. He ignored the big barrel of water boiling, full of rags and sheets even now. It added little warmth to combat the foggy atmosphere.

As fast as the public appeared enraged by the torture of the crew, the winds had changed and Captain Clarke was once again being hailed as a bastion of good will. If Matthew ever got the chance, he would kill Clarke. He wanted Harris dead too, so very much. But the thought of that brute set him to trembling and tearing up like a baby. When nightmares plagued him, Matthew had thrown himself against the walls of his room in terror. He learned his lessons well, the size of a man doesn't give you any idea of how much of a monster he could be. Matthew promised himself, he would get better with a gun. He would never be taken again.

Father Arturo distracted Matthew with stories of his personal travels from Spain to Rome, where he studied for the priesthood. His family was well off and expected him to rise to power in the church. But God had other plans for Arturo. Waylaid by robbers during his travels, a poor man rescued him even though his family were suffering lean times. Arturo never forgot that selfless kindness. His father settled no little gold on the man for the sparing of his son. Later Arturo's father was not so overjoyed when that same son took vows to minister to the diseased and desperate. So instead of treading the golden halls of the Vatican, Arturo crossed the world to find his calling among the miserable souls that ferried the world's wealth in the great sailing vessels.

As the months passed, Matthew's spirit was soothed by the unrelenting faith the brothers expressed as they labored and the sameness of his days. Their kindness never wavered even as their patience was tested to its limits. He occupied himself in a relentless focus on weaving bits of string and rope into Solomon knots. He wore the bracelets he made or left them lying around the place for the errant sailor to pick up. Some days he blocked out his surroundings completely in a desperate effort not to remember his experiences. No war, no ship, no Harris.

When he was not intent on the one thing he learned on the hell ship, Matthew helped the brothers do their work around the place. Soon his own hands were raw from the endless chore of washing sheets and boiling bandages. He hammered nails into ill-fitting planks to patch the leaking roof and cover gaps which let in chilled air. Some days he would sweep the floors and Father Arturo would warn the brothers off while Matthew completed turn after turn through the sanctuary, his mind lost to the movement of broom back and forth.

As suddenly as he became lost in repetitive actions, Matt would be reconnecting with everyone again, listening to their stories and absorbed in Arturo's history lessons.

Time lost all meaning to the healing man. Matthew considered remaining inside the confines of the Father's mission forever. He was safe there, hiding from a world filled with enemies wanting his demise.

*****

1877

Matt dangled from the end of the rope, his chest scrapping against the side of the cliff. He would have more than a few abrasions after this was done. Sweat from exertion and the sun baked rocks stung his eyes. He was pretty much climbing blind, depending on his pony to get them up. The man hitched to his back was shorter than he, but at least twenty to thirty pounds heavier. That he was unconscious added to the problem of getting him back up to the narrow trail. Blood from a bullet wound in the man's shoulder soaked the back of Matt's shirt.

He braced his legs once more and pulled himself up another foot. His old pony continued to take up the slack, holding steady against all the cropped eared evidence suggesting he was a killer to anyone fool enough to mount up. Matt's gloved hands scrabbled for a hold onto the crumbling edge of the drop off. He was suddenly dragged over the top a few feet more before Croppy snorted in relief and returned to nipping at the sparse grass. He lay for a moment gasping for breath, the man a dead weight on top of him.

After a minute or two, Matt squirmed out from under the body. He got his canteen from Croppy's saddle and used a little to moisten the man's parched lips. The bullet had passed through the body so Matt poured a little of his last few swallows of whiskey in the holes then used his one clean bandana and a few strips of rawhide to tie down for a bandage. The man had lost a lot of blood and his face was pale and sweaty with shock. Now they were up here, Matt hoped that the darkening sky wouldn't bring a storm before he found some place to hold up with his unconscious charge.

Croppy snorted and pranced away as Matt pulled him over to the body. His legs were no longer trembling from the climb, so he figured he could hoist the man into the saddle and get moving. The old pony's notched ears were flat and teeth bared. But he stood perfectly still under the weight and didn't kick Matt in the head as he tied the man's wrists to the saddle before mounting up behind him. There wasn't any sign of a horse running down the trail ahead of him, so Matt wondered where the man's horse could have gone. Thunder rumbled in the distance. He knew a night in the rain would probably end the man.

They journeyed for maybe an hour before the first icy drops fell. Matt covered the man with his slicker and put his own wool lined jacket and gloves on. The temperature dropped abruptly. If he had to make do with the sparse trees they would both probably get struck by lightning. Thunder echoed around the mountains and Croppy threw up his head and refused to move another inch.

"Come on you mule headed nag. You won't stay dry standing around out here."

Dismounting, Matt grabbed the bridle and halter alongside Croppy's jaw and pulled him along the narrow trail he had been following. The old horse kept baring his teeth and snorting all the while but didn't kick or bite. The trail was too wide to be an animal track, so perhaps there was a cave or cabin at the end of it. At this point a cave would be grand as long as it was free of bears.

Lightning cracked overhead, scaring the hell out of man and horse. Some distance away a tree sizzled as it burst into flames, but the sudden torrent of rain thankfully overwhelmed the fire. The first flash of light left the impression of some kind of structure ahead. Relief was quickly replaced by caution. Whoever ambushed the old man could be hold up there. For the first time in months, Matt pulled his gun.

He took time scouting the area thoroughly before approaching the building. Just because he didn't see any lights didn't mean a killer couldn't be watching from the dark windows. Someone wanted this man dead. They could still be around. It wouldn't be the first time and the thought of that incident made him shiver. His mother used to say someone was stepping on your grave when that feeling crawled up your spine. So he made himself wait until his nerves settled before he circled the cabin and eased along the west wall to the door.

He nudged the door open with his gun barrel. Rusty hinges resisted the intrusion, but the door swung back against the wall. He eased down and went in low, the pounding rain covering his first cautious entry. Lightning lit up the night and the sudden flare exposed no other intruders, though it was a near thing not to fire his weapon at the shadows! Matt holstered his gun. He had the impression of a table with a lamp atop it. He hoped there was oil. A crude fireplace was the last image from the lightning flash. It would do. So he hurried out to bring the wounded man in.

First he carried the old man inside and laid him on the floor nearest the fireplace. Matt stripped the saddle and his meager supplies from the pony. He hobbled old Croppy in the wind protected space between the cabin and the rock wall that rose up behind it. He hoped the battered overhang resembling a back porch would be enough shelter from the lightning. Matt wanted to take him inside the cabin, but Croppy hated barns, stalls and men in general. He tied on the feed bag with the last of the oats he'd bought in Silverton. He left the horse rolling his eyes and staring him down with laid back notched ears. There would be hell to pay come morning for leaving him out here, but having a right fit thrown inside and stomping on his patient wouldn't do.

Matt felt his way to the fireplace, finding fairly dry kindling already laid and a rusted crane and trivet. He took flint and steel from the inside pocket of his coat and set to work. He was relieved when smoke disappeared up the chimney and the tiny flame grew. Thank goodness there was wood already stacked against the wall. He was dogged tired and still needed to bed down his feverish patient.

Matt removed the man's outer garments and boots. He discovered a crude bunk and took the dusty blankets for a good shake in the open doorway. He dragged the bunk over to the fire, then lifted the old man atop it, tucking him in against the damp. A further search of the single room turned up kerosene and a few cans of beans and peaches. Someone obviously used the place from time to time. The cans weren't old and the blankets weren't moth eaten. He filled the lamp and lit it. Unpacking his gear, Matt got coffee going with collected rainwater. After checking the shutters were secure, he latched the door. When the room warmed up he shucked off his coat and hat. After a while the scent of frying bacon and potatoes filled the room.

He checked the old man's wound, cleaning the holes out by lamp light. All that time lying in the open and then the ride just might do him in. Matt hadn't heard any shots the last days riding in the mountains. He would have thought the sound would have carried to him. The fact that a fat roll of bank notes and silver dollars remained in the money belt around his waist, was a sure indication of why the old man was bushwhacked. But Matt couldn't just leave him. Nobody should have to die alone.

Exhausted, Matt finally set down to the unsteady table to eat. The crude chair rocked on its uneven legs until he sat in it. A can of beans and peaches bulked up his meal. Those rare peach slices were much appreciated. There wasn't any money left for pleasures like these right now. The bread, cheese and the rest of his meager stores would have to be rationed until he could get out of this situation. Matt needed to get a job before his last few dollars were gone. He wasn't always welcome at smaller homesteads, because of his worn clothes and nightmare pony. He usually worked the ranches as he traveled, but steered clear of the mining operations. The rowdy mining camps were filled with rotgut and greedy men scrabbling over silver and the few women that dared to try and survive there. A law abiding man had to keep close watch on his property and worry too much about a bullet in the back. Those places brought back bad memories.

Luck graced him once more when he discovered a thick bar of wood leaning in a dark corner of the room which he used to keep the door firmly shut. The latch was no more than tattered rope over a nail. Now there would be warning if those bushwhackers showed up. He built up the fire considerably before he bedded down on the floor, hopefully to get a full night's sleep without dreams. Mindful of that money belt, he tucked it in next to the man. He didn't need to be accused of theft. The old man had been shot from the front. He wasn't wearing a gun. The horse and rifle he should have had was gone without a trace. Matt slept with his rifle close at hand by the fireplace. Contrary as ever, dreams did not disturb his rest at all during the remainder of the stormy night.

The rain pummeled the cabin for three days. Random holes in the roof left puddles on the floor. Matt had to move his bedroll twice to avoid the irritating splashes of cold water startling him from sleep. The old man's fever worsened and for a while Matt was sure he wouldn't make it, but he was a tough one alright. For the time being his fever was down and his breathing deep. Maybe he would wake up soon and tell Matt where he should take him. Right now his most dangerous task was seeing to his right irritated pony. No, Matt didn't shiver as he cautiously made his way across the muddy track to the back of the cabin.

*****

Croppy was staring at him with white rimmed eyes and teeth bared in righteous indignation. The wall eyed grulla's hide gleamed in the sun from an intensive currying. His stubby tail and scant mane were free of tangles and burrs. Matt wiped the sweat from his face with his forearm. He surveyed the result of his labor with a faint smile. Croppy was hobbled for the moment, otherwise he would be trying his best to kick in Matt's ribs. Pulling that rawhide loose was going to be an adventure.

The cowboy smiled as he ran toward the cabin, dodging the snake like lunge of the ewe necked devil. He wiped his boots along the porch edge before he went into the cabin.

He checked his patient, still resting quietly. Matt was pretty confident whoever tried to rob the old man had given up. The weather should have further discouraged them. It must have been a pretty cowardly bunch, since the money wasn't taken. He had met few men in this country not tough enough to climb down there and take what they killed for.

Matt foraged some wild greens and snared a couple of rabbits on his fifth day. The old man had swallowed some of the broth off the meager stew Matt had boiled up and kept on the fire. Now there was more confidence the man would recover. Matt settled down to eat, grimacing at the lack of salt and seasoning, but grateful all the same to not have an empty belly.

After cleaning up he stepped outside again leaning against the wall to roll a smoke. It wasn't a regular habit, but he was bored. There weren't any old magazines or newspapers in the cabin and Cloth of Gold was memorized from constant use. Sooner or later he would get back to Silverton or Denver and get some new reading material. Maybe he would winter up here in this cabin. With a little patch work it could be secure. Even with the signs of regular use, he would hope who ever laid up wintered someplace else. He never liked staying over in Denver for the winters. But logic demanded he learn more about surviving the weather before taking the chance on living alone during snow season.

Matt was taking his last drag on the butt, when Croppy's head swung up, ears pricked forward. He turned to face the trail they had come in on. A horse whinnied, not close by yet. Matt reached inside the door and picked up his rifle, stepping back into the dim room.

Croppy snorted and backed up near the cabin wall, nostrils flared and teeth bared in antagonistic greeting. They waited.

Three riders emerged from the stand of aspen around the cabin. A boney shouldered old man lead the procession, his eyes lost in wrinkles and weathered face. A white handlebar mustache dropped over his thin lips, tainted yellow from tobacco. There was a girl riding behind him with copper hair, shot through with gold and red sparks from the sunlight. Another man rode up beside the girl. He took off his hat and shook the water off it, then mopped his face with a handkerchief. He leaned toward the girl and said something to her. Her chin went up and she shook her head, stubborn refusal obvious on her face. He flushed pink and jerked his horses' reins hard, riding up next to the old man. He was blond, hair cut close in the eastern way, thick and curling with pomade. Even from inside the cabin Matt could see the vivid blue of his eyes.

"Hallo the house," the old man called. "We smelled the smoke. We're lookin' fer someone."

Matt stepped out onto the porch, his rifle held casually in both hands.

"You're not looking for me mister. I don't know you," he growled.

He saw the men straighten in their saddles, suddenly wary.

"Now wait a minute son, don't get testy. My names Gil Jones, foreman of the Rocking Falls Ranch on the plain below these here mountains. We're lookin' for the boss man Will Bethencourt."

"He's my father. I'm Sarah Bethencourt. Please have you seen any strangers or heard anything? He's been missing near a week."

Sarah moved her horse ahead of her companions, ignoring Gil's upraised hands to warn her back.

"Please sir, have you seen anyone? How long have you been here?"

"Hold on a minute lady. How do I know you're really who you say you are? A pretty face don't mean you can't be up to no good."

"Wait just a minute. Who the hell...," the blond put his hand on the butt of his sidearm and Matt's rifle shifted, aimed dead center.

"Stop it Kevin. The man is right. He doesn't know who we are. Here, look here."

Sarah reached inside the collar of her shirt and pulled out a locket dangling from a silver chain. She lifted it over her head, anxious hands fumbling her first attempts to get it untangled from the long copper braid.

"Here, look inside. There's a picture of me, my father and mother."

"Toss it over here," Matt demanded.

He caught the locket out of the air with his left hand and stepped back inside the cabin. He recognized the man as the same one lying in the bunk behind him. The hair was darker, but the cut and heavy mustache was the same. Sarah was a little girl posing between him and a thin fragile looking woman. Obviously Sarah took after the woman in looks. Matt closed the locket and stepped outside.

"Miss Bethencourt, your father's inside."

"Thank you!" Sarah quickly shifted to dismount.

"Hold on, hold on. He's been hurt and still unconscious!"

She was already pushing passed him while he was speaking. He heard her worried cry and then she was calling Gil to come to her.

Matt stepped aside as the two men stepped down from their horses and rushed the cabin. He followed, rifle trained on their backs. While the trio hovered over the bunk, Matt pushed the shutter back letting in more light and waited for their next move.

"That's a bullet wound Miss Sarah and looks like he's been bashed about the head too."

While Gil and Sarah were examining the wounds and black bruises, the one called Kevin turned to Matt, his hand once more sliding to his holstered gun.

"Mister, Mr. Bethencourt was carrying a lot of money, just where did you say ..."

"I didn't say," snapped Matt. "Whatever he had on him is still on him. I'm no thief."

"Kevin! Dad's money belt is right here."

"What?"

The blond's face was blank with shock. He stared at Matt in disbelief, his face once again rosy.

"Well damn mister. I don't know what to say. I'd like you to accept my apologies. It's been such a worrisome time. We've been just at the end of our rope."

He took off his gloves and offered Matt his hand. His smile was disarming. Matt looked him in the eyes and saw nothing but a rather embarrassed younger man trying to impress a girl. He shook the proffered hand. Kevin sighed in relief and couldn't stop the side long glance in Sarah's direction.

'No harm done, Mr. ...?"

"Oh, Harlan. Kevin Harlan. I really am sorry for my crude accusations."

"Apology accepted Mr. Harlan, though you aught to know accusations like that can get you shot out here. My name is Matthew Travers."

"Really pleased to meet you, Matthew. It's a good thing you came along when you did. Sarah was out of her mind with worry."

"Glad I could help."

Matt sat his rifle down and motioned Kevin to the table.

"Take a load off. Coffee's hot."

"Good I could use a cup." Kevin sat down and poured the thick black concoction that Matt called coffee. He couldn't stop the grimace at the bitter taste, however.

"Sorry about that. You might want to water that down some."

Kevin grinned and his face got all rosy again.

"Well it is rather strong." He laughed then and gratefully took the canteen Matt was offering to pour some water in his cup. Matt was rather embarrassed himself. He wasn't much of a cook.

Sarah finally moved away from her father's side and approached the table.

"Thank you Mr. Travers, thank you so much. I'm sending Gil for the rest of the men. One of them can ride for the doctor."

"There's a doctor around here?"

"There's a doctor out at the Wimbly Ranch. Some cousin of theirs from Silverton," Kevin interjected.

"He came to assist their cook. She's having a baby and always has trouble. I hope he's still there."

"Well there's not much grub left. I got some rabbit and wild greens in that pot on the fire. And there's cans of beans and peaches."

"That's alright Mr. Travers. I'm sure we can add to it." Sarah gave her father's savior a smile.

"You men sit and have your coffee. I'll take care of the horses," Matt offered.

"Thanks Matt, but Gil's the one needing rest. Old bones, you know."

Kevin laughed and followed Sarah outside. He didn't see the look of disgust that twisted Gil's face.

"Young upstart," Gil grumbled. "Thinks he knows it all."

Matt hid his amusement as Gil got up and stumped out to take care of his own horse. Sarah rushed back in and began unloading the saddlebags she dumped on the table.

"We'll just heat these up," she said laying aside a bundle.

"They're biscuits," she grinned at Matt, "and you can drop this into the pot with your rabbit."

She tossed Matt another bundle which turned out to be half a cooked rabbit.

"I've also got some cheese and bacon. There is a little bit of flour and salt too."

Matt dropped the rabbit into his pot and added the little sack of salt.

"I have a few snares out since morning. I should go check them. A couple more rabbits wouldn't hurt nothing."

"Alright Mr. Travers. When you get back supper should be ready. Oh, Mr. Travers?"

"Matt will do mam."

"Ah yes. Well Matt, thank you again for saving my father."

"It was purely an accident mam. I'd been tracking this hawk's flight and just happen to look down and see your father lying on this ledge. I wasn't sure if he was alive, so I climbed down. It's a good thing Croppy's such a good cow pony. I'd never got him up otherwise."

"My father had fallen off a cliff!" Sarah's face paled during Matt's description of her father's rescue.

"Sorry mam. I didn't mean to scare you. It was about an hour back that away."

Matt pointed to the east and Sarah paled even more. She sat down and Matt quickly pour her a cup of coffee.

"Here Miss drink this. I didn't mean to cause you more upset."

"What's going on in here? Sarah are you alright?"

Kevin's voice startled Matt so, he almost reached for his sidearm, which was still lying on his bedroll. He stepped away from the table to cover the move. Trust some girl with eyes the color of new pennies to make him forget he was surrounded by strangers. He turned to face Kevin and spoke more sharply than he intended.

"I thought she was fainting."

"Father had fallen off a cliff!"

"What? Sarah honey, you're white as a sheet."

He hurried to her side and took her into his arms, murmuring whatever nonsense women wanted to hear when upset.

"Leave us alone a minute, will you. You didn't have to tell any horror stories." Kevin was frowning at Matt over Sarah's shoulder.

Sarah tried to object but Kevin's arms tightened more pressing her face into his neck. It was Matt's turn to stump outdoors. He snatched his coat off the nail by the door and was gone into the trees. Kevin shushed Sarah's protests and continued to rub her shoulders. Soon he was kissing her forehead and cheeks. He kissed her lips, deepening the kiss fairly quickly. Sarah began to struggle.

Kevin, my father and the door's open. What are you doing, stop it!"

She pushed him away.

"God Sarah, I'm sorry. You just go to my head. You're so beautiful. Every time I hold you. I'm sorry, really." He grinned sheepishly and backed away from her.

"Forgive me? Please?"

She was frowning and it took a heartbeat longer than normal for her to give him a shaky smile. He was peeking at her from under long pale lashes, his eyes imploring.

"Alright Kevin. I didn't mean to snap."

"I know honey. You're tired and I'm being a bore. Here sit down and drink your coffee. I'll get the rest of our things. Once the doctor gets here and your father's home you'll feel better."

Sarah watched him go outside. Then turned her thoughts to putting together a meal.

Mr. Travers surprised them all leaving her father's money on him like that. His frayed store bought clothes and that horrible looking animal they saw near the cabin marked him as a very poor man. Most cowboys were working for a dollar a day. Sarah wondered if the long scar on his cheek was gotten in a knife fight. The oddest thing was the spectacles he wore. The lenses were smokey gray and seemed to wrap around the sides. She had yet to see his eyes, but he didn't appear to be short sighted, certainly not when holding them off with that rifle.

Contrary to most cowhand habits, his guns were well oiled and clean. He moved quiet too. For all the inconsistencies his integrity was obvious. He looked directly at everyone he spoke to, catching their eyes. Sarah's father always remarked on men who wouldn't or couldn't. She tried to think what color they could be behind those gray lenses. His skin was tanned and his hair was deep brown, near black. It was shaggy and curled around his ears and shoulders. It was a mess but he obviously made regular use of a straight razor.

She had no fondness for beards, although her father favored them. He used to tease her by giving her bushy kisses. She would squeal and make a break from fiery cheeks rubbed red by the wiry hair. She loved her father but his ideas of affection usually left her feeling more than ever, she should have been a boy.

Sarah placed the sliced cheese on the table and supplemented Matt's dented plates with their utensils. They could eat soon as the biscuits were warmed through. Sarah raked the hot ashes over her tightly wrapped treasures and stepped outside. She was standing under lowering skies when Matt returned. She never heard his passage through the woods. He glanced her way but went inside. She should go in and dish up his food. Her father would surely give the man a job after all he'd done for him. When Sarah got inside Matt was hunched down by the fire eating from his battered plate. Two skinned rabbits hung from a hook off the mantle. Kevin and Gil came in behind her heading straight for the freshened coffee. She quickly dished up the stew for the other men and turned out the biscuits. Making her own plate Sarah sat down in the wobbly chair at the table. She passed the plate of cheese to each man. Matt got up and opened two cans of peaches and passed it around.

"I have to make sure to come back up here and replace what I used. Somebody obviously stops off here from time to time."

"Might not be friendlies. Kind of off the usual trails," Gil commented.

"Yeah I did wonder on that. Was only luck I found it in that thunderstorm. Almost passed it by. It would have been bad for both of us with the lightning and all."

"Yep, Mr. Bethencourt was lucky you came along. We might have never found him. How did you manage that anyway?" Kevin looked curiously at Matt.

"I noticed a couple of red tails seem to be keeping to my trail. I was looking for their nest when I noticed him. Didn't see any sign of his horse though. Thought that odd, but didn't have time to look around. The storm moved in real fast and the lightning got bad. Even after the rain stopped I couldn't see trying to take him anywhere in his condition. He seems to be resting better. We should all turn in early tonight anyway. It looks like another storm maybe brewing."

"I'll go along with that suggestion young feller. I'm plum tuckered myself. If I'm gonna ride down the mountain I'll need to start out at dawn to get to our base camp. Hope you're wrong about that storm though. It could last another couple a days and Will needs that sawbones."

There wasn't much said after that. The group addressed their hungry middles and didn't leave any left overs. Matt put the rabbits on a spit to roast before he spread his bedroll on the floor.

Sarah looked beyond him to see her bedroll setting atop her saddle by the bunk. Gil rolled his blankets out on the other side of the fireplace and was soon covered up with his hat over his face. Matt followed suit leaving his rifle propped against the fireplace at his shoulder, his gun holstered on his hip because there were strangers all around him now. Kevin and Sarah looked at each other and shrugged. In a few minutes they were all lying down. Kevin positioning himself beside her.

Matt lay awake a long time under the cover of his hat listening to the rustles and sighs as everyone settled. He hoped the man could travel in a few more days anyway. It was good there were folks looking for him and could take over. But it was still nerve wracking to be around people he didn't know.

It seemed like minutes later Matt opened his eyes to watch Gil tiptoe out into the dawn's light. Kevin rolled out of his blankets with a groan and stumbled out the door behind him. After a while Matt stirred and stoked up the fire, putting on the coffee. He took a can of beans, heated them in the skillet and tossed in the last two biscuits. He went to the door calling out to Gil, startling both men.

"There's bean and biscuits on the table for you. I'm thinking you got a long ride and its real cold this morning."

Gil strode into the cabin peering up into Matt's face. He grinned and patted the younger man's arm.

"Thank ye kindly son. It's pretty nippy and a full belly will help me along."

With that he sat and wolfed down everything in a few minutes. He drank two cups of coffee before putting on his coat. Sarah set up at that moment yawning and stretching.

"Oh Gil why'd you let me sleep so long. You need breakfast at least."

"It's alright Miss Sarah, Matt here rustled me up some grub and stuffed me right good. I'm on my way."

He walked over to the bunk and kissed Sarah on the forehead.

"Don't you worry yourself honey. I'll be back with the boys to get Will home and the doc should meet us there."

Sarah smiled and hugged his neck.

"I don't know what Father and I would ever do without you Uncle Gil. I love you."

"Girl don't start all that mush. Let me out a here boys. I'll be bawling like a dogie in a minute." Gil laughed and stepped out. Kevin called after him.

"You be careful ole man. Whoever waylaid Mr. Bethencourt might still be around!"

"Only if they want a belly full a lead." Gill called back slapping his sidearm. He stepped into the saddle and turned his chestnut cow pony into the trees.

Sarah cooked breakfast and spent the remainder of the morning tending her father. Kevin was talkative, however she noticed Matt spoke very little. After seeing to his horse, he ate with them but retreated to the doorway to read. He put on those odd four lens spectacles when the sky cleared and sparkling sunlight filtered through the trees.

"How long have you been reading that book Matt?" Kevin asked. The blond was leaning forward in the chair squinting at the dog eared yellowing pages. "What's it about?"

"It's called Cloth of Gold, Henry Aldrich. It's a book of poetry."

"Aldrich, Aldrich. Hey that the same fellow who wrote A Story of a Bad Boy?"

Matt looked up and nodded. "The very same. I never read that one. Got this in a dry goods store in Denver a few years back. The clerk tossed it in my kit. Said he was done with it."

"And you still reading it after all this time? You really must like poetry." He rocked the chair in his amusement.

"I do." Matt returned to his reading.

"No offense Matt. It's just you don't look like a poetry reader to me."

"Kevin."

"Ah, Sarah I was just kidding around."

"It's fine Miss Bethencourt. Reading material is hard to find in this country. Poetry was a gift of sorts."

"What do you mean?"

"Friend of mine in the war had an interest in poetry. When he got killed, I got his belongings. He had no family to speak of so I kept his written efforts. I planned to have them published one day, but..."

Matt's expression darkened. He frowned and returned the book to his saddlebags.

"Pardon me mam."

He picked up his hat from the saddle on the floor and stepped out the door.

"Wait Matt. I'm sorry. We didn't..."

"Ah Sarah, let him go. We didn't do anything. Probably just bad memories."

"We should apologize. It wasn't right for us to pry."

"We didn't pry. You asked a question and he answered. He could have begged off. He'll get over it. Don't get so worked up."

"I don't want him to leave angry Kevin. We owe the man."

"Well honey, why don't you give him some money now and send him on his way."

"We can't do that. He saved father's life. Father would want to meet the man that risked his own to save him."

"Maybe so, but I still think you should pay the man and let him go about his business. Gil and the boys will be back soon enough. Beside's we don't know anything about him. Maybe us showing up disrupted his plans."

"Plans? What possible plans could he make? He could have left father to die and stolen the money. We would never have known. Instead he treated his wounds and stayed with him."

"Maybe someone else got to Mr. Bethencourt before him. It would be easy to save him and then cash in later. It's no secret in the territory your father is well off. Between the Army contracts and his interest in the silver mines, he's worth ten times what's in that belt."

"Kevin, this is ridiculous! There's no logic..."

"Ridiculous, we've only got his word he pulled your father off a ledge!"

"I won't listen to this nonsense."

Kevin left the chair and grabbed Sarah by the shoulders.

"Let go of me. How dare you!"

"Sarah, Sarah damn it! Calm down. I'm just asking you to think! Stop it girl. Your father's life's at stake!"

Sarah gasped and stopped pushing at Kevin to stare at him.

"Sarah honey, I'm not saying not to be grateful. I'm just saying be careful. Don't let gratitude blind you to what's possible. We don't know this man and he could have plans. We have to protect your father until he can take care of himself. I may be paranoid, but better safe than sorry."

"I'm, I'm sorry. You're right. I guess I've been so happy I didn't want to think the worst thing..."

"It's okay Sarah." Kevin said, pulling Sarah into this chest and stroking her hair. She rested against his shoulder. He caressed her until the shivers ceased. Finally he stepped back and looked into her face.

"You still mad?"

She had the grace to blush scarlet.

"No, I'm sorry Kevin. I misjudged you. I thought you were...well, never mind forget it. I need to consider what you said. Help me Kevin, help me keep an eye on Mr. Travers."

Kevin gave Sarah his most dazzling smile and hugged her again.

"You bet honey. Don't worry I'm staying right by your side."

She hugged him tightly and sighed when he buried his face into her hair. Sometimes Kevin was so gallant and other times she wanted to hit him over the head with a pan. Now was not one of those times. He had a point. Matt Travers was a stranger. Maybe only what he appeared to be, a good man in a country where law abiding were few. But to protect her father she could not let her softer emotions interfere with caution. If the man did not look so...ah well, enough of such thoughts. Her father came first. Travers could take care of himself.

*****

Matt took deep breaths of the rain washed air, cleansing his mind of dark memories. The battlefields and his punishment aboard the Sunrise cursed his rest even after these many years. He had met other men broken by the war, wandering aimless, sometimes so damaged they were helpless to do more than drink or drug themselves to death.

He could still see his mother's face, stern and resolute, when he returned home. Father had already acquired the regulation uniforms, a pale gray almost white outfit with scarlet trimmings. He was busy organizing his overseers and servants to manage while he was away. Benjamin, his wife and children had just arrived from their home in Georgia. Their youngest brother Leo, at sixteen, would be left behind to care for the women. Matt had feared the coming confrontation that was to leave him further outcast and he was not wrong. His father was struck speechless, then shut himself away in his office. Benjamin had responded with fists, until the women intervened. His mother, shaking with tearful frustration, showed him the door. She berated him in French, the language rarely spoken around the plantation since his grandmere had passed.

"What foolishness. The disgrace. How can you defy family over something like this? How could you think of pointing a gun at your father or your brother? No son of mine could do this!"

But he stood his ground, followed his principles and plunged into a hell. He lost that naive belief that blood honorably sacrificed would cure the country's ills. He discovered Northern sympathizers usually had as much disdain for his views in regards to the Negro question as his family. Every bullet fired may have struck his loved ones. He fought at Antietam, surprised to survive with painful but quickly healing wounds. The lack of effective leadership in the Union army appalled him. Men died by the hundreds, by the thousands.

Matt returned home after the conflict relieved to discover the house intact at least. All around was evidence that the war had encroached onto home ground. Pits from shelling covered a field that had always been filled with tobacco. Poorly marked graves were the only thing planted there now. Graves even edged one of the side roads, the men all buried where they fell. Former slaves worked in the fields closer to the house. Only foodstuff was being grown. The stately trees once lining the drive to the front door were only stumps or splintered caricatures. It was a miracle the house remained in one piece.

He knocked on the door, Ann answered. Deprivation had bowed his sister-in-law's shoulders and left her gaunt, even her hair faded to gray. She spat in his face. He slipped his current letter under the door. Two days later Leo knocked on the door to the room Matt rented in a small hamlet about ten miles from home. Leo was twenty, face lined from the weight of his burdens. His eyes were bleak as he stared into Matt's eyes. The message was short and brutal.

"Father died at Gettysburg. Mother collapsed after we got word. She was dead a few months later. Ben could not come home because he would have been shot for spying. We got his last letter in '63. He was moving from one regiment to another as men were killed off. He must be dead. We don't know if he ever received the last packages we sent. The only thing keeping Ann on her feet is the children. Why in heaven would you think anyone here would wish to look upon your face?"

"I'm so sorry Leo, more than I can say. I'm sorry."

"Were you at Gettysburg killing our father or prancing around New York preaching your negroism? Was it a bullet from your gun killed him?"

"Don't you think I worried over that every minute? I wasn't the only one with family and friends on the other side. What else could we do but try to stay alive. I couldn't fight to keep people like cattle! Father branded people Leo. You don't treat a human being that way!"

"Who gives a damn about your conscience, you murdering swine. You raised your hand against your own. If you had not the courage to hold onto our birthright, you should have stayed run off like the coward you were. We would have been better off for it! God knows, I'd kill you now if I could."

Matt turned away from enraged features, so like his own. The young man's face was flushed and his eyes were flooded with unshed tears.

"Leo please..."

Matt turned back to an empty hallway. He reported back to his unit and performed his final duties immersed in the Indian conflict. Any remaining belief in justice was completely eradicated after seeing the new atrocities fed by fear, lust for gold and revenge on both sides. Like former slaves, some tribes took sides in the conflicts. It availed them nothing but broken treaties, starvation and incarceration. He could see the day when whole tribes no longer existed.

A clash with rebelling warriors garnered him a slashed face and a bullet creased skull. The doctors were amazed that there was no penetration or fracture, just an awful bloody gash and blindness. After months recuperating his sight slowly returned.

Matt mustered out, returning to New York, continued his studies and opened a law practice. He was working hard at making a new life. But drink smothered the pain during many nightmare ridden evenings. After spending one night drinking in a local tavern, he had been caught in the crossfire during some street brawl and new round of nightmare began. His precarious sanity was threatened more than anything previous on the horror ship.

Lost in memories, Matt sat beneath a pine, cushioned by the needles that carpeted the ground. Images rushed before his eyes and his head began to ache. Looking back he couldn't believe how naive he'd been. Freedom for the Negro was followed up with new sanctions against them. For many life was no different than before. And the Indians were losing ground every day to confinement and disease. Were his sympathies twisted in that regard as well? He had fought them regardless of his beliefs. How much sense did any of it make?

McNamara surprised him, coming in person to escort him out of San Francisco. Matt recalled his terror, the shame, of sitting in the carriage trembling as they went to the train station to begin his journey back to New York. Months later he sold McNamara his part of the business and left for the territories. Ignorant of life in the wild, he endured and came to appreciate the places away from civilization.

In all the years since he went his own way, shunning most company. More often than not an object of suspicion because he was not well off. He worked at whatever was at hand; mill rider, bronc buster and even plowed land for nestors in exchange for food when they allowed him. He had little pride left about such things. His occasional letters home were never answered. Of course they wouldn't be, but Matt continued to flog himself with that decision to continue writing in hope.

Reading his book always brought to mind Jimmy Stanwick. An uneducated street ruffian, Jimmy had shown him the badly spelled poetry he wrote. Matt made the mistake of taking an interest, helping the boy learn to read and write properly. Jimmy purchased a book of poetry with his first pay. But the day came when Jimmy lay screaming for his mother, bleeding in a muddy ditch with no aide to be had. Jimmy never knew who his mother was, but he using his last breaths begging her to save him before Matt put an end to his pain.

All those memories crashing around inside his skull, filled his head to bursting. He could feel the pressure building behind his eyes. The doctors swore the headaches were not caused by anything but his imagination. They performed thorough examinations of his skull for any abnormalities, as if palpating his head would tell them what was happening inside it. Matt was convinced the literal blinding pain would eventually put a permanent end to his sight. When it happened he would do for himself what he did for Jimmy that horrible day.

Right now he needed to take his laudanum and sleep. He never used it unless he got one of these bad ones, not wanting to wind up stealing to feed the addiction. So many of the men he fought with came away with horrible attachment to this concoction. Every time he was wounded, the fear of getting a permanent desire haunted him. It was bad enough he wound up drinking heavily. Matt walked back, squeezing his eyes shut against the batches of sunlight breaking the heavy foliage. Even his spectacles weren't much help when the headache came on.

Sarah was sitting on the floor by her father's side when Matt stumbled into the cabin. His face was beaded with sweat. He was grimacing against the pain. She jumped to her feet alarmed by his appearance.

"Mr. Travers! What's wrong, what's happened?"

"Nothing, nothing. Headache real bad," he mumbled.

Matt tossed aside his bed roll and dug through his saddlebags until he found the little bottle secured in a small leather pouch and wrapped in cloth. His hands shook as he fumbled it loose from the bindings. Taking a deep breath he allowed only two drops of the tincture to fall on his tongue. He would sleep through the night and probably drag around the next day until the lassitude wore off, but anything was better than the ax blade slicing into his skull. He fumbled the bottle back into its wrappings and knotted the strings of the pouch tight. He would not forget to seal it away and keep it secured in his saddlebags. A quick drink from his canteen washed the taste away. Intent on arranging his blankets, Matt was startled by Sarah standing over him.

"Mr. Travers, will you be alright?"

Matt couldn't hold back the flinch from the sound of her voice. Everything was so loud.

"Alright after I sleep. Honest lady I just need quiet awhile. Got shot...war...head hurts. Sleep please."

Sarah was still watching, worry escalating as Matt collapsed onto the blanket. He was shivering as if he were cold. She didn't know if it was the medicine he took or if he was feverish. He pulled his hat down over his eyes and curled up. She knelt down beside him to ease the second blanket over his shoulders. He curled up tighter and rocked himself. She backed away and stepped outside to warn Kevin that Mr. Travers was ill.

Kevin had insisted on scouting the area to insure their continued safety. She thought he was being overly paranoid. Mr. Travers opportunity for wrong doing was surely passed. Honestly, If Kevin was showing off for her, he was only causing her to rethink their possible engagement. Should he not be here at her side protecting them? A man needed common sense to survive in this country and the exasperating man didn't seem to have it right now.

Sarah paced back and forth for a while. She went back inside to fix an early supper. Mr. Travers never moved other than the occasional deep sighing breath. Sarah ate a solitary meal before resuming her pacing exercise before the cabin.

Finally Kevin stepped into the clearing. She ran over to him and hissed.

"Where have you been? I've been worried sick."

"Sarah, you wouldn't..."

"Shh...not so loud."

"What's wrong?"

"Come over here."

Sarah tugged him back toward the stand of pine.

"Where were you?"

"Like I was trying to tell you. I tried to follow Travers. I got lost."

Kevin flushed a deeper hue than usual as he showed her his lost puppy face.

"Lost!"

"Yeah, lost. I've been trying to get back here for more than an hour. He must have figured out I was following and laid a false trail. Why are we whispering?"

"Mr. Travers is inside."

"What, when did he do that?"

Sarah rolled her eyes and crossed her arms to keep from smacking Kevin.

"You have been gone half the day Kevin, not an hour! Mr. Travers appears to be very ill. If I understand him, he was wounded in the war. He took medicine and asked for quiet while he slept."

"Medicine, what kind of medicine?"

"That isn't any of our business Kevin. The man was in obvious pain. He's asleep. I don't think you could get him up if you tried. If you are so suspicious, why did you go off on this scouting trip through the woods and get lost? The man has done nothing to warrant anymore of these speculations. I made supper. Come in and eat. We are going to be on short rations until the boys get here. You can tell me about your scouting trip in the morning."

Sarah turned away, dismissing the entire matter. She was tired and now had double the worry. If Mr. Travers was down for another day, she would have to find his snares. Kevin never handled hunting on the ranch very well. Needless to say he was proving less than skilled for ranch life. Rabbit would not be on the menu at home for the coming year if she had anything to say about it.

"Wait a minute, Sarah. Look I'm sorry, alright? I'm trying to be, well you know. I'm sorry I worried you."

"I apologize if you think I was harsh Kevin. I'm just tired and anxious. That man saved my father's life, evidently at plenty of risk. We don't need to worry about anything but getting home. I don't expect you to have all the answers to this situation. But we can't go off the rails. Innocent til proven guilty remember?"

Kevin moved close and hugged Sarah. She was stiff in his arms then sighed and relaxed.

"Honey I've had a hard day and so have you. Let's just relax and try to enjoy the evening. The moons full tonight." He bent to kiss her. Sarah allowed his lips to lightly brush against hers before pulling away.

"Kevin I'm too tired and worried. How can you expect me to relax when you yourself remind me the stranger who saved father might still be a danger? Now both men are down. I've paced back and forth for hours worrying about you. I'm exhausted. I'm sure you you must be tired from your ordeal."

Sarah pulled away turning toward their shelter.

"Remember, keep it down Kevin," she admonished just before she entered the cabin.

Kevin removed his hat to brush his hair back with his fingers. He pulled hard until his scalp tingled, then stalked in behind her. Sarah sat his plate on the table before settling down on her bedding. She pulled off her boots and lay down. She watched through narrowed eyes and raising ire as Kevin scraped his plate clean before shoving it away. He removed muddy boots, dropping them on the floor, the showy spurs clanging. He tossed them over his bedroll before stretching out on the floor beside her.

"Good night Sarah. I'm sure you'll feel alright in the morning sweetheart."

She twitched, but kissed him on the cheek and murmured 'good night'.

Kevin turned over a number of times, complete with grunts of dissatisfaction against sleeping another night on the floor. Exasperated, Sarah turned her face to the wall beneath her father's bunk. Tonight she absolutely would not spend any more time worrying about the current situation. Gil should be back in two days at most. Father would get well and Mr. Travers could have a job, which he seemed in sore need of. He didn't strike her as the 'reward hunting' type. But a job over the coming winter they could do. She did not know what to think about Kevin. He was entirely too inconsistent with his affections. I'll keep you safe one minute and off lost in the woods the next.

Sarah's anger kept her awake half the night. The sun's appearance found her stiff and more irritable than before. She lay there, surprised to see Mr. Travers sit up and stretch. He gazed around the room, blinked and smiled at her. He sighed and ran his fingers through snarled hair.

"Sorry about last night. I get real snappish when the pain comes."

"I understand. I didn't know how to help you. That frightened me."

"Didn't mean to scare you. Got shot during an Indian raid. Still pains me now and then."

"Oh, I understand. It's alright. I just wanted to help."

Matt got to his feet, swayed a moment and stretched once more.

"You couldn't do anything. I just have to sleep them off. I'll probably sleep most of the day too."

"Can you keep it down? I'm still trying to sleep," Kevin admonished from beneath his blankets.

"Sorry Harlan. I'm stepping out anyway."

Sarah watched Matt leave using the table and the walls for support. He didn't look too steady at all. She checked her father's condition. He still seemed to be sleeping comfortably. She hoped he would awaken today. After folding her bedroll, Sarah left the cabin for a moment of privacy in the woods. She washed hands and face from her canteen before returning to see about breakfast. There were plenty of beans and cold rabbit. Mr. Travers had left the broth to stay hot over the fire. Sarah hoped her father would be able to eat it. She eventually divided the remnants between the three of them. After setting the filled plates on the table she rousted Kevin out.

Obviously unhappy, Kevin scrubbed at his face and sat down at the table. Sarah took her plate and settled in her place by the bunk. They were eating silently when Matt returned. His hair was wet and he appeared well scrubbed. His face was bare of spectacles for once. Sarah was surprised by the brightness of silvery gray eyes against his tanned complexion.

"Where did you find enough water to wash up?"

"Well actually I just wandered a different trail into the woods this morning and found this little seep along the mountain behind us."

"Please show me where. I'm dying for a bathe."

Matt chuckled, rocking back on his heels. He braced himself on the table, took his plate and lowered himself carefully by the fireplace. He scraped some of the lukewarm beans into his mouth before saying more.

"There's not enough water trickling down from that hole for a bath Sarah."

Matt continued to chuckle as he focused on his food.

Sarah stared, rather bemused. He was handsome when he smiled.

"Well I'm going to move the horses to better grazing," Kevin said, pushing away from the table. He stepped over to Sarah and caught her chin between his fingers.

"You can show me the way to that water later on Sarah honey."

He pressed his lips to hers, tightening his fingers when she pulled back.

Matt got to his feet, leaving the partially eaten meal on the floor.

"I'll take the canteens to refill. Come on if you're going Miss Bethancourt."

He was out the door and into the trees before Sarah and Kevin parted. Kevin winked at Sarah before he left. Sarah ran in the general direction Matt took, her entreaties for him to wait disregarded. She was breathless and angry when she finally caught up with him. He was filling the canteens.

"You can wash up after I'm gone. I have to water the horses."

"It was Sarah a little while ago, Mr. Travers."

Matt felt his face grow hot. He stoppered the last canteen and turned to her.

"I meant no disrespect, mam." He tipped his hat in her direction and hurried away.

Sarah caught herself in time to prevent a righteous swear word from escaping. Men surely got on your last nerve. Growing up around cowhands tainted her vocabulary early. Her mother insisted on finishing school attempting to eradicate their influence. The results were dubious at best. Even now when Sarah was thwarted all the hands knew it. She could cuss a blue streak if her mother wasn't around. That a ragged saddle bum would dare treat her like that. The nerve of some people. Ignore her one minute and smile at her the next, then run off in the middle of her conversation.

Remembering her father, Sarah scrubbed as best she could and returned to the cabin. Matt was in front, currying that pitiful looking nag he rode. She stood in the doorway watching while taking apart her braid and attempting to comb out the tangles. Cobby tried to bite or kick his curry comb swinging tormentor every chance he got. It wasn't long, however, before Matt had him saddled and mounted up. Cobby was so battered, you wouldn't think he had the strength to buck like that. He sunfished like a dervish. Surely that wasn't helping

Mr. Traver's headache!

"I'm going to ride out and check for sign. Whoever shot your father may have hold up like we did. Better be cautious. Won't be gone long."

"I'll be fine Mr. Travers. I am armed and Kevin is nearby." Sarah couldn't help her frosty tone. The man was staring.

Matt didn't say anything for another long moment. She wanted to retreat into the cabin when he abruptly departed without another word. What an insolent...

Sarah finally noticed Kevin was nowhere in sight of the cabin. She stomped inside and just missed putting her foot into Matt's plate. Mumbling under her breath she picked it up and sat it on the table rather forcefully. Serve him right if she served him the congealed beans for supper.

Matt rode along the narrow trail leading from the cabin, noting the tracks the horses made while it was fairly muddy. He singled out Gil's cow pony and rode on eventually breaking through the brush onto the cliff side trail. On the surface Sarah Bethencourt was the kind of girl his family would not have approved of. He recognized the signs of finishing school manners. Yet her hands were work roughened proving she loved the outdoors and the responsibilities of ranching. The weird getup she was wearing would have given his mother a fit. He had not wanted to be caught staring, but for sure she looked to be wearing pants underneath that short dress. The clothes weren't fancy either. Homespun, a vest and denim skirt from the looks of it. But that Spanish sombrero caught his attention. It had been resting against her back, like a picture frame for those copper curls come loose from her plat.

What she saw in that fickle, smooth talking Harlan he'd never understand. Goes to show education doesn't mean much if you don't use it. Harlan was a study in contradictions alright. Cocky one minute and helpless the next. Always blushing and wheedling when caught out in the open. Her father would disown...ah stop that thought, it brought too much pain. No, no one deserved that. If Miss Bethancourt married that tin plated, dime novel pretender, she would be back east in a hot minute with everything her father owned sold off for city life.

He continued his ride unable to shake the image of Sarah standing in the doorway with her copper sparked hair loose over her shoulders. Even after two nights in wrinkled clothes she was beautiful.

Cobby looked over his shoulder at the tormentor. The reins had gone slack and he refused to continue along the trail unless forced. There was nothing to eat on this rocky path increasing his ever present disgust with tormentors in general.

Beautiful. That's what Sarah was, beautiful. Matt looked around the mountains. He heard the hawk's cry and shading his eyes, searched the sky. It fell like a stone into the deep, brush strewn drop off alongside the trail. The screech of triumph echoed as the hawk suddenly rose into the air, prey dangling helpless from its talons.

Birds were to be envied, free to roam the skies, eat and rest at will. They lived, taught their offspring to fly and died. Matt was sure somewhere inside them it all made sense. They were, and that was all, no heartbreaking decisions just life without doubt. Being human was awaiting the next onslaught with trepidation. He remained on watch, until the hawk disappeared up the mountain. Suddenly, the wind picked up, causing Matt to hunch his shoulders against the chill during the return trip.

*****

End of Part 1

PROJECT S.E.E.

Space Exploration Explored

THE CARHAYAKEN RING

By Tachyon Node Staff

Abstract

The Carhayaken Ring is a theoretical torus structure made mostly of earth and metal. The disciplines most likely to contribute heavily to its design, development, and construction would be physics, mechanical engineering, nuclear and photovoltaic systems, agriculture, Urban Construction, LEED, 3D printing and environmental sciences. For this paper the ring has a diameter of 10 kilometers and its intended purpose is to provide 1) Data for creating an eventual larger Carhayaken Ring, 2) an alternative option to sending humans to other planets, 3) provide extraordinary real estate for humans to use, and 4) an additional means to the perpetuity of the human species. The Carhayaken ring may be placed anywhere in the Solar System and within any orbit around any planet. It may also be placed in its own orbit around the Sun.

Introduction

The Ring should be of significant size as to house a large and diversified work force. Its position in space will determine its usefulness in providing a platform for a variety of missions: Interstellar launches, deep system exploration, Asteroid mining expeditions, and exoplanet searches. The ring's thickness is measured in kilometers with a shell of metal, dense earth, and rock.

Currently, Earth is using up its natural resources at an alarming rate. Population has passed the 7 billion mark and current means of addressing food and water shortages are inadequate.

The idea of creating extraterrestrial real estate that would greatly and potentially enhance the quality of life for humans is intriguing. Population crowding would be the ring's immediate problem to solve. The access to an abundance of solar materials would solve resource scarcity for the ring and the planet Earth.

Creating a Carhayaken ring presents a multiple set of problems. First and quite obviously is that a construction project of this size has never been done on the planet Earth. The ring's construction and completion would have to be an International effort. Secondly, Earth would have to take an aggressive approach in completing the project. Even though current technology may be used in constructing the ring, said technology would have to be adapted to space travel. Also, some common mining techniques can be used be may have to be tweaked to work in a space environment. Mining and building is something humans have done for hundreds of years. Robotics would be heavily relied upon, but there would still be a need to put humans into space. Constructing an entire ecological, self-sustaining object of celestial size is something humans have never done.

For the Ring to be successfully completed, humans would have to cooperate at a level never before reached. The International Space Station was a test. The Carhayaken Ring would be of humankind epic proportion. Though several nations and International agencies would be able to start, construct, and complete the project, it would be of the upmost importance that all nations contribute to the construction of the Ring. There has to be International buy in either financial, materially, technologically, and/or with personnel.

System Model

The Carhayaken Ring is a ring torus with a diameter of 10 kilometers. The ring's body would be two kilometers thick with the outer shell consisting of 500 meters of rock or concrete. Interior composition would be material collected from asteroids. The ring would be segmented into 16 pieces with water 20 – 25 meters thick in between each piece acting as a cushion and lubricant. A sleeve-disc combination would be placed surrounding the space between two segments.   The pressure between each segment should be high enough to keep the water from 1) freezing and 2) boiling. The segmentation would allow for the ring to expand, contract, and warp (to a small degree) without damaging the ring as a whole. Each segment would contain dozens of spheres made of rock, concrete, or metal. Each sphere would house huge populations of people, animals, vegetation, life-support, and equipment.

Gravity within each sphere would be produced by centrifugal force. The Spheres would be divided into banded areas at different axis and latitudinal lines. The banded areas would rotate a different speeds, depending on their latitudinal location to create an equivalent of .5 to 1 Earth g.

The added benefit of the gyroscopic forces generated by the bands would help each segment maintain position within the ring assembly.

Problem Statement

There are a few problems to consider with constructing and maintaining a mega-project such as the Carhayaken Ring:

- Materials gathered
    - Where?
    - How much is needed?
- Construction technology
    - Will current disciplines work?

o   Adapting terrestrial hardware to extraterrestrial use?

o   Efficiency and how much is good enough?

- Personnel
    - o   Skill level of workers?
    - o   More reliance on automation?
- Transportation technology
    - o   Current Rocket Science?
    - o   Advance Propulsion?
- Life support technology
    - o   Air generating?
    - o   Farming?
- Emergency preparedness
    - o   Containment breach?
    - o   Water and Air contamination?
- Ring assembly integrity and Movement
    - o   Allowing for flexing and uneven gravitation and inertial forces?
    - o   Orbiting transfers?

Solution

The ring segments will be created from materials gathered from the asteroid field. Once we overcome the technological hurdle of capturing and transferring asteroids to different orbits, we can start constructing the ring. Current construction techniques should work and can easily be transferred to off-world construction.

Equipment will have to go through some developmental stages for adaptation for vacuum operations, personnel will have to be trained and properly equipped. Current screening procedures for astronauts will have to be greatly revised. Safety protocols will have to be revised, as well, accommodating mid-level skilled workers and there will be more reliance on robotic technology.

Today's rocket technology is currently adequate, however, for efficiency in material delivery and transportation we will have to start using more exotic propulsion systems such as ion drives and VASIMR systems. Time to complete a Carhayaken Ring is irrelevant,

Habitat Rings

however, more advanced technology will be employed when it becomes available.

Once a ring segment has been completed, interior building should immediately commence. Each segment should be self-sustaining with power, water, propulsion, and life-support. Power will be generated initially from nuclear sources and then, eventually, switched to 100% photovoltaic and supplemented with battery storage. Population will be housed in large spheres embedded in each segment. Water will also be stored within each segment, but also can be drawn from the water section between each segment in the event of an emergency. Propulsion of each segment will mainly be used for attitudinal control and helping with initial orbital transfers.

Most segment control functions will have to rely on automation. Computers and robotics will control critical mission functions such as life-support, segment position control, power distribution, system repair, and orbit position. Humans would assist in final component assembly and wiring. Most system programming and monitoring will be done by humans. Cooking, some cleaning, some system maintenance and repair, furniture construction, and customizing of creature comforts will also be done by humans.

Initially, food, air, and water will have to be shipped to the first segment during construction. Afterward, all life-support needs can be supplied from the completed Segment One installation. The majority of water will be supplied from captured asteroids and comets. All necessary building materials will originate from captured asteroids. Propulsion fuel may come from Jupiter, Saturn, the other large planets, and a by-product of electrolysis for creating oxygen from water..

The propulsion system for each segment will consist of several components: Gyroscopic, Chemical, Ionic drive, and VASIMR systems. Positional stability will be maintained by the gyroscopic forces produced from the Population Spheres within each segment. Also, each segment would have a main command "deck" and Engineering section to control and monitor all functions and features of each segment. One Segment, in concert with the other segments, would control the entire ring assembly.

Emergency Preparedness will consist of individuals carrying a container of emergency air at all times during the initial interior construction phase of each segment. Because each segment is covered in a thick shell of concrete, radiation exposure will be at a minimum. The Nuclear power generators would be maintained on the outer most portion of the segment and could be jettisoned in the event of an inevitable meltdown. Most emergency power needs could be supplied by photovoltaic systems so the loss of a nuclear power generator in a given section of a segment would be negligible overall. A segment could also burn liquid fuel such as hydrogen.

LEED techniques would be established as an integrated normal practice throughout the build out phase of each segment. During the first few years of a segment being inhabited, emphasis on efficiency and energy saving would be placed when necessary. Each housing unit within a given segment would be supplied with emergency air, food, and water for several years. Training in fire suppression and atmosphere breach repair would be taught at different levels. All workers would be required to go through the basics. Once families are introduced and established, basic Emergency Preparedness, Safety, LEED, and Emergency procedures would be integrated into all levels of education.

Air generation will rely on a number of processes. Farming, traditional and other means, along with park and natural environments would be established. Vegetation within these designated areas would be used as a natural filter for scrubbing out CO_2 and supplying oxygen throughout the segment spheres. Electrolysis for energy generating would also generate oxygen as a by-product.

As mentioned earlier, gyroscopic forces generated from Spheres needing to simulate gravity will help maintain overall ring integrity. The Sleeve-Disc combination pieces will allow for some movement along the y- and z-axis of each segment. Different Advanced Propulsion Systems will be used to fine tune segment position and when used in combination of other segments help with ring orbit transfer.

Conclusion

Potentially, Earth's overall technological knowledge seems to be at a level high enough to undertake constructing a modest Carhayaken Ring. New exotic alloys will not be needed nor would radical building techniques have to be developed. Adapting current terrestrial construction methods to extraterrestrial usages would not require extraordinary measures. Getting International cooperation would probably be the most difficult. We already have several companies pursuing Asteroid mining and there are more than enough civilian companies capable of conceiving, developing technology, building equipment and tools, and launching everything, including people, into space.

Related Work

Dyson sphere
https://en.wikipedia.org/wiki/Dyson_sphere

What is a Dyson sphere?
http://earthsky.org/space/what-is-a-dyson-sphere
Dyson sphere: What are the odds of an alien megastructure blocking light from a distant star? By Anders Sandberg
http://www.ibtimes.co.uk/dyson-sphere-what-are-odds-alien-

megastructure-blocking-light-distant-star-1525042

How to build a Dyson sphere in five (relatively) easy steps
http://www.sentientdevelopments.com/2012/03/how-to-build-dyson-sphere-in-five.html

What is a Dyson Sphere? by FRASER CAIN on SEPTEMBER 19, 2013
http://www.universetoday.com/104919/what-is-a-dyson-sphere/

Torus
From Wikipedia, the free encyclopedia
https://en.wikipedia.org/wiki/Torus

Centrifugal force
From Wikipedia, the free encyclopedia
https://en.wikipedia.org/wiki/Centrifugal_force

Rotation around a fixed axis
From Wikipedia, the free encyclopedia
https://en.wikipedia.org/wiki/Rotation_around_a_fixed_axis

Gyroscopes
http://www.gyroscopes.org/behaviour.asp
http://www.real-world-physics-problems.com/gyroscope-physics.html

Asteroid Mining
http://www.planetaryresources.com/
http://www.space.com/30213-asteroid-mining-planetary-resources-2025.html

Water in Space
https://medium.com/starts-with-a-bang/does-water-freeze-or-boil-in-space-7889856d7f36#.qi7aq4llv

VASIMR
https://en.wikipedia.org/wiki/Variable_Specific_Impulse_Magnetoplasma_Rocket
https://www.youtube.com/watch?v=Glg6pWwezEU
http://www.adastrarocket.com/aarc/VASIMR

ION Drive
http://www.nasa.gov/centers/glenn/about/fs21grc.html
http://nmp.jpl.nasa.gov/ds1/tech/ionpropfaq.html

The Carhayaken Ring
PROJECT
One Earth
Billions of humans
One human dies
We survive

EXODUS EXTRASOLAR

FOLK TALES
ERU
COMIC REPUBLIC
3
FEAR ITSELF
ERU
OUT NOW
EZEOGU
EZEOGU
IKECHUKWU
WWW.THECOMICREPUBLIC.COM

I Know Something You Don't Know

Moshe Prigan

He met her at an exhibition of paintings in the local museum. She spent a lot of time looking at a small particular picture.

"I painted it," he commented noticing her interest, and then he apologized for distracting her.

"This one is awesome," she said, pointing at a small charcoal sketch of two girls sitting back to back on a dune among tall grass. Below was scribbled I Know Something You Don't Know.

"I'm flattered that you think that. Thank you."

"My name is Briana Cole. I teach art in high school," she said, offering a handshake.

"Dave. Dave Bonham," he said. She had a delicate palm with elegant fingers that he wanted the handshake to linger longer.

"Cup of coffee?"

Her smiling face acknowledged him. They went downstairs to the restaurant and he ordered black coffee while she asked for ice cream. When she gathered her silky long hair into a high bun he said he would like to paint her and she laughed.

"Do you paint?" Dave asked.

"I'm so exhausted after school that I just have no energy to do something, the more so to paint. I prefer going to exhibitions.

"This exhibition is my first public appearance since I lost my wife. I paint to overcome my grief."

"I'm sorry to hear that," she said.

"My wife got killed in a train accident a year ago, leaving me with my little 6-year old girl." He pulled a small picture out of his brown wallet.

"That's my little treasure, Maggie."

They chatted the whole evening and Dave learned that she was single.

"My ex-boyfriend tried to paint me but, the painting didn't even resemble me in the slightest way. I wasn't black and comely enough," Briana laughed.

It was the first time he felt some envy at the thought she had a boyfriend.

"How long have you been dating your boyfriend?"

"We've been together four years." Briana noticed he became restless.

"Didn't you think of marrying this guy?" Dave asked.

"I didn't want to get married, not then, and not to him. We just wanted to hang
around."

"What were you doing the day you met him?" Dave asked.

"He actually met me, but why do you ask me that? I feel some jealousy in your tone." She leaned toward him. He liked the scent of her hair. She had milk chocolate skin and big shining eyes. Dave enjoyed looking at her.

"Maybe. See it as a compliment."

"I think you're ..."

"Falling in love," Dave cut her off. Briana burst into laughter and then touched his wrist.

"Do you remember the earliest moment of your life, Bri? I hope you don't mind me calling you Bri," Dave said.

"I don't. My earliest …? What kind of question is it, Dave?"

"Try it."

"Who can remember" she said, waving her hand aside. She straightened her blouse over her pert little breasts.

"I don't want to sound conceited but I can. There's something seared deep in my mind."

"What is it?"

"I remember kissing you."

There was a look of surprise on her face at that moment.

"Are you hinting that we met up somewhere before?" she frowned.

"Yes, I am, we did."

"I don't think so and I don't remember that. Nothing comes to my mind right now."

"I do. I first kissed you when you were a baby, two years old. I was six. It was at the Baby's Health Center."

Dave leaned back in his seat, tapping his fingers on the polished table.

"No one would be able to remember himself at such an early age. You're just imagining that," Briana said.

"I'm not, but I can't prove it."

"You're so funny, Dave. I like guys who surprise me with some mystery."

Dave signaled at the waiter for another cup of coffee.

"And what would you remember from us meeting today?" she teased him.

"I think I already declared it, didn't I?" Briana smiled.

"You're lucky to have such a memory. I wish I had one like yours," Briana said. "I tend to forget things."

"I mostly tend to remember bad things."

"But you just told me you were falling in love with me. Isn't it a good thing to take away?" Briana winked.

"I wish I would remember. I do want to."

"You dare not," she said, hanging her head aside.

"And what's your earliest bad memory that you'd like to forget?" Briana asked.

"Me sitting in a stroller, aged four, pushed by my older brother. He bumped it into a wall and I hit my head."

"You have quite amazing memory."

"And I thought you would say you were sorry I had bumped my head," Dave laughed, pushing Briana slightly. She pushed him back.

Then they embraced.

"I had an extraordinary memory in school," Dave said. "I could recite the Song of the Sea and Song of Deborah, but one summer day I forgot my daughter's name."

"How that happened?" Briana asked.

"We were at the beach and I called her Nicky instead of Maggie. I called twice but she didn't answer. Sitting close to me, a fat red-faced woman said: 'Why doesn't she answer you?' I felt confused."

"You painted a little girl encircled by broken letters, forming, as I now understand, her false name."

"Exactly. You have a good eye, Bri."

"And the painting with children and their decapitated parents, all sitting erect as if posing for a photographer ..."

"You mean the one called Broken?" Dave interrupted her.

"Yes."

"What about it?"

"I felt uneasy. That's a horrific painting."

"I painted my worst memory, Bri."

"What is it, if I may ask?"

"I remember the day your mother was killed."

"What?" Briana almost screamed. She shoved her chair backwards.

"I was four years old when she got killed. We lived not far from your parents' house. You were the only black family."

"So we grew up in the same neighborhood," Briana said. "But why don't I recognize your face? Did you graduate Bridgeport high school?"

"I didn't. My mother couldn't afford that."

"Why not?"

"She had to stay home to take care of her three children, me and my brother and sister on one income alone."

"Where was your father?"

"My father was executed."

"Oh My God!"

"I saw him during his last moments. I remember me sitting on my mother's knees, crying. He was the first white male executed in Idaho."

Briana approached her chair and took his face between her hands.

"Why? What did he do?"

"Homicide."

"Jeese. I'm so sorry for you, Dave, and for your poor mom. Does she still live there, in Bridgeport?"

"We lived there until the homicide case of your mother. Then we had to move on."

"What did it have to do with my mother?"

"I'm sorry Briana, but my father murdered your mother."

Dave, noticing she was losing color, pulled out several wet tissues from the tissue box holder on the table and wiped her face, gently, slowly, as a sculptor making the last corrections of his work. He ordered a bottle of cold water and held it to her lips. She took small sips. She was slouched way down in her seat.

"We're two lost souls bumping into each other on one cold evening in a gallery," Dave said.

The restaurant workers started putting chairs onto the tables. Some of the last people just left.

"I have got to go. A long day is waiting for me tomorrow," Briana said. "I am going to take my class on a trip to the beach."

"I'll call and tell the school principal you fell ill."

"You're so kind, Dave.

"Would you wear a bikini?"

"With all the pupils around? No way." Now she fully smiled.

"Then I'll see you after tomorrow. We'll go for a swim, only us." Dave said. "We'll meet on the dock at five."

The humid night swallowed them up.

*

When Dave drove down the highway leading to the beach to meet Briana on the dock, he figured he would just have to wait about fifteen minutes for her. The beach was empty and the sun was already low. He had been waiting on the dock for her until the sun kissed the sea.

He drove to the gallery. She wasn't there.

After a week without a word or call from her, Dave decided to drive downtown and cruise the streets, to places where school teenagers hang out and shop. He entered the city mall and saw two young girls looking through the window at the clothes in a fashion store. They were talking loudly about buying new garments. Dave turned to them.

"Excuse me, young ladies; do you know a teacher named Miss Briana Cole? She teaches art."

"Sure, she's our teacher," squeaked the blond one, moving aside her tousled hair.

"She fell sick and has been taken to Saint Paul Hospital," the other girl said.

Dave sped through the maze of streets, ignoring several red lights at pedestrian crossings. In the reception, he was told that Briana Cole was resting at Ward B, Room 5.

He found her asleep, looking sedated. She was lying in a small room, with a window facing the Bridgeport dock where they were supposed to have met. He pushed a loose strand of hair away from her face and touched gently her cheek. Bri opened her eyes. As she saw him, she started weeping. Dave tried to soothe her, saying when he realized she hadn't shown up at the dock he figured something had happened.

She signaled to him with her finger. He put his ear to her mouth.

"I found my dead mother," she whispered and pointed at the bedside cabinet. Dave straightened himself up. The headlines on the front page of Bridgeport Evening Star read: "Human bones found on Beach Dowson." He fully opened the folded paper.

"Two school girls, being on a school trip to the area, found human bones in a dune. They were later identified as belonging to Miss Rose Cole who was murdered two decades ago and whose body has never been found. The killer, John Bonham, confessed to killing her but refused to reveal where he buried her body. He was charged on strong circumstantial evidence and was executed by lethal injection shortly after trial."

Dave took a deep breath.

"Remember my small sketch in the gallery with the two girls sitting on a dune?" Dave whispered in Briana's ear. She nodded.

"I painted the place where your mother's body was found. I titled it I Know Something You Don't Know." She slanted a look at him.

"Did you know something about my lost mother?" she asked in a low voice.

"No," Dave shrugged.

"It took about twenty years to find her, and she was found one day after we met."

"Strange things happen, Bri."

"You've been painting the sad stories of our families. You touched our lives with the same brush."

"They've come to an end, eventually," Dave said.

"Things got solved since we met," Briana said.

"Then it was a good thing we met."

Her smiling face acknowledged him.

###

COMIC REPUBLIC
#1
GUARDIANPRIME
GENESIS
WE KNOW HIS MIGHT...
IT BEGAN HERE.
M'ART
IKECHUKWU
AWELENJE
NOV 2015
COMIC REPUBLIC
WWW.THECOMICREPUBLIC.COM

Psyche
A Story of Virtual Law

Brandon Hill

Today was Friday, the end of her standby shift. This meant that Kate would be shuffling off her uniform for the weekend. Though there was never any real reason to take it off -nanomaterial could mimic any fabric and was self-cleaning, on some paranoid level, a part of her felt like she was not so much in control of it, as it was trying to take over, like she was in a constant battle of wills against the A.I. that governed its components. What worried her most was how it resisted whenever she did remove it, as if it hated her for rejecting the comfort and protection it provided. It felt like pinpricks in each of the pores of her skin, as if hanging on for dear life, making a conscious effort to remain on her, even after she gave the mental "release" command.

It was a fear she only shared with Dr. Galt, the League psych evaluator. What a coincidence that her train of thought would swerve in this direction during an evaluation. And no doubt Dr. Galt would pick it up, either on the brain scan running through her biocomp or on his own, being the off-planer and psychic that he was.

"Tried to sneak away from our little session again, have we?" The doctor asked in his slightly exaggerated, almost-German accent. The chief had to have told him about her previous attempts at shirking her appointments; it was the only way he could have known. She had hoped that she could have done so again, but the chief liked to keep a tight leash on his subordinates. The reminder popped in her field of vision today just as she had finished lunch: priority one, mandatory. The doctor was kind enough, but his voice, for its out-of-place accent, was oily, snake-like, and did little to endear him to her. But she bore him no ill will; after all, he did go out of his way to be nice.

"I hope it wasn't because of me." The doctor rubbed his tiny hands together as one of the four pseudopods that grew from his hunched back manipulated the readouts upon the touch screen of his OffBoard peripheral.

"No. Not you," A flat, mildly sarcastic tone managed to escape her voice, even though she was being earnest. "You'll excuse me if I don't like you probing into my head."

"Oh, surely it's not so bad," Dr. Galt protested, with a laugh that was just as dissonantly unsettling as his voice. "Procedure and all that, especially when you've got so many bionics attached to you."

"Yeah. Procedure," Kate echoed, unable to move much more than her arm to bring the cup of Darjeeling tea to her lips. Tendrils of nanofiber ran like cascades of straight black hair from her uniform, wove together at their ends like braids, and were shunted into multiple jacks on several terminals. All there was left was to sit and wait while the doctor took his readings. "Thanks for the tea, by the way."

The doctor nodded cordially, and continued his work. No questions were asked; there was no need. He could see inside her mind as easily as he could see readouts from her OnBoard as it fed data into his brain via the INplant at his right temple. And this composed the entirety of the evaluation in all its inane boredom.

"Seems that everything is in order," the doctor said at last, stirring Kate from her state of between-sleep-and-awake. He touched a key sequence on his periphery, and the tendrils retracted from the terminals, flowing like a river running on rewind, into her suit's mass reservoirs with an audible snap. The empty teacup rattled in her hands upon its saucer. "And that will be all for me ... until next month, that is."

With little more than a noncommittal sound, Kate rolled out of the couch. Her steps were ungainly at first, but her biocomp quickly compensated as it awoke from standby mode. She managed a brief smile at the doctor as she left the office, but had no intention of showing up next month. And to make sure that the chief would not call her out on it, she planned to have a talk with Jackie about the League mainframe, schedules, and the fudging thereof.

The ghost of an itch ran across her skin. She scratched reflexively. God, she would be glad to get this thing off, and move around without digital checks and balances made on her every bodily function! Now, there was only a brief detour for calibration and diagnostics, and then she would be home sweet home, enjoying beer and barbecue packs.

Kate paused, suddenly as a ping ran through her biocomp and caused a tremor in her skin. The words, PRIORTIY MESSAGE: REPORT TO DIRECTOR GARRETT, shone in bright red, flashing their urgency in her line of sight.

"Damn," Kate said under her breath. Had he started reading her thoughts now?

It was worse, she discovered all too quickly.

"Your regular shift has been extended." The director had said the words she dreaded. Her insides were one part a lead weight, and one part seething with vitriol. But she maintained a steady poker face; duty first, after all. It was always duty first with the League, but she could not help the thoughts that ran unbidden through her mind.

What the hell are you thinking?

Do you have any idea how much I look forward to taking this thing off?

Don't you have about a hundred other A-Class enforcers on tap?

"What's the assignment?" Was what she asked.

"The MAGI," Garrett said. "I'm sure you heard of them?"

With a thought, Kate's biocomp scoured the I-Link and supplied her with the relevant data about the organization. There was, surprisingly, very little. They were considered a terrorist group by the League simply because they opposed them (paranoid much?). Their list of "sins" consisted mostly of data infiltration and industrial espionage on some pretty sophisticated mainframes.

Kate frowned as her feelings of indignation deepened to something that was almost like hatred. This was grunt work, pure and simple, and far beneath an A-class. "What's wrong?" She asked, disguising her disdain under a veneer of snide stoicism, "techies can't handle a few super hackers? Finally caught one in the real world, and you need me to babysit him?"

"No."

Oh, right. Humor and sarcasm were completely wasted on the director. His tone was as flat as yesterday's soda, colorless as his office: no plaques, pictures, or personal effects of any kind, save the League half-star symbol, mounted prominently behind him in brass behind his featureless mahogany desk. The man was practically a robot.

He touched a sequence on his OffBoard, and Kate's biocomp signaled an upload with a shrill chirp. Immediately, data integrated itself with her memories.

"Those are your orders," the director said with finality as a familiar name stood out the data. The face to match that name suddenly came through the door, her blue skin and snow-white hair unmistakable.

"Mukai?" Kate rose from her chair quickly to greet her friend. "When did you come back to Earth?"

Mukai smiled kindly and bowed. "An hour ago. It is good to see you again, friend Kate. I look forward to working with you." She spoke in Glossiu, the language of her world, meaning her INplant had not been outfitted with an English translation matrix. Her transfer to Earth had indeed been a swift one.

"She will be working with you on this case," the director announced.

"You're joking, right?" Kate quipped. Perhaps no English module was a good thing, she thought, or else Mukai might have taken her words as an insult. She gave her a quick glance, but Mukai's decorum was better than a marine's.

"No. She has the technical expertise you will need. And you two have had a good, albeit brief working history, and a longer personal history. You know this is a good pairing, Lieutenant."

"Krid," Kate swore under her breath. Robot though the director might have been, he was always right.

***

Their first stop was supposed to be at an ATM across town, but a real-time update had changed their destination to the old transcontinental Bridge: an abandoned project from the more optimistic previous century, where squatters had set up a miniature city over the years. Apparently, a new suspected access had been made at a local restaurant that she was familiar with, but details, as expected, were sketchy. Mukai had always been few of words, but she had obviously never driven a car through subspace; the way she flinched as the ghosts of traffic passed harmlessly through their car where there should have been lethal collisions was amusing, but not unexpected. Subspace was the best way to travel if one were in a hurry. Kate found herself unable to suppress a laugh as Mukai staggered out of the car onto the parking lot, making profuse apologies. Kate reassured her friend that her disorientation was normal, and then led the way up to the shops, bazaars, parlors and dives on the Bridge's second tier.

"First time on enforcer business?" Kate asked. Though Mukai wore no English translation matrix, Kate had one for Glossiu, though she knew the language fairly well. Still, a matrix helped for the big words.

"It is my first time directly working with one on Earth," Mukai said with a nod.

"Well, it's good to have someone helping, even if you're an import," Kate admitted. "I mean I don't know what could've possessed the director to deputize an off-planer from a completely unrelated organization, but..." Her voice trailed off as they neared their destination down the crowded thoroughfare, its old sign suspended from overhanging rooftops.

That was when she realized that the sign was actually on. The unusualness of this alone gave her pause to just stare. The name "Pink's" shone in neon cursive, the same color as the name, as if it had never spent those last ten years burned out and unrepaired.

"Under new management it seems," Kate observed aloud, then saw that the windows of the facade had been repaired, and a fresh coat of varnish graced the entrance door. Even the latch was new, shining with the near-gold sheen of polished brass, where the old one was rusted solid and had barely been hanging onto the door frame.

She stepped inside, and the unexpected and pleasant scent of newness and sawdust greeted her. The place looked like some itinerant fairy had taken up light housekeeping reversed the effects of time. The many and sundry photos of the music groups who played there in the past were still posted on the walls, but amidst a backdrop of fresh white paint newly applied to the sheetrock, free of yellowing and graffiti; the furniture, tables, menus and order terminals were also brand new.

"If I wasn't on duty…" Kate said. With a wistful sigh, she steeled herself for the task. ahead.

"We'll be checking the order terminals first," she told Mukai. After showing her credentials to the surprised, but acquiescent manager, she set to work.

During the investigation, Kate realized, much to her chagrin, that she was hungry – small wonder there, since the director hadn't given her the opportunity to grab a snack before heading out, and she was long overdue for dinner. And that the VIRsense matrix encoded into the order terminals for OnBoard access did not help to diminish her appetite. Soon, after being bombarded by the simulated sights and smells of a hundred menu items, she could stand no more. She jacked out of the system and located Mukai, who was now five rows down and still hard at work. I'll leave her to it, she thought, personally wanting to just get away from the torment of food.

She snapped the terminal's face plate back into place as her jack retracted back into her suit, then prepared to make an order for something to drink while the investigation continued, still decidedly, annoyingly unfruitful.

A minute later, she was sipping on a glass of iced Green Dream, inputting parameters of real world legwork into her biocomp. She was admiring the finished half of the ongoing repair job on the rear stage, when she noticed someone appear from behind the curtains.

"Hey!" Kate hurried down the way, and through the barricades that warned of the danger. "That's a microbot area; get out of there. You could mess up their programming; they might turn this whole Bridge into-"

She paused in her tracks as she approached the stage, and then slowed to a walk. A smile had erupted upon her face, as well as the face of the person across the way.

"Aly!"

"Sis!"

Kate's mind went back to a conversation with a coworker from about three years ago, and the photo that accompanied it, still hanging on the wall above the booths in the eating area. She had been right. Alicia did look almost exactly like her, but with shorter hair, highlighted in purple, and with a star tattooed beneath her left eye. It had been years since they'd seen each other, until they were reunited during an investigation in Mukai's home dimension of Gaia nearly two years ago. Kate's younger sister grinned as she sat on the edge of the stage, her legs dangling. She wore all black, and for a moment, Kate thought it was another enforcer uniform. But as her sister reached out and took her hands, and then hopped to the floor where they shared a happy embrace, she noticed that there were no line patterns or half star insignia - then it dawned on her that it was a diffusion suit, for safe interaction with on-duty microbots.

"Nice coinkeydink, meeting you here," Alicia said.

"I used to come here all the time, actually," Kate replied. I actually saw you perform a few times, back before you went platinum."

Alicia sighed as she ran her gaze across the breadth of the stage, the billions of microbots still hard at work, doing repairs one molecule at a time, un-rotting the wood, re-weaving and re-coloring the curtains, and un-rusting the metal. "Yeah, it brings back memories; that's for sure. Broke my heart when I came back from tour and saw the kridpile this place had become."

"Well then," Kate said, "if you're not the luckiest girl in all the worlds. Seems like the new owner liked this place the way it used to be."

Alicia gave a wry grin. "Who do you think bought it?"

Kate gave an explosive laugh that surprised even her. "You're kidding! "You bought this dump?"

"Won't be a dump for long," Alicia said. "Soon, this'll be the hottest night spot on the Bridge."

"No krid?" Kate scanned over the half-completed stage, a jarring contrast of decay and newness being born from dilapidated sections. "New sounds like before?"

"Revue of up-and-coming talents from every plane known to man and off-planer."

Kate couldn't help but grin. It was like the nanobots had rearranged the muscles on her face. "Wow. So I guess you've been busy since the last time I saw you,"

"That was a year ago," Alicia reminded her.

"A year ago?"

"Yep."

"Seriously?"

Alicia nodded. "Time flies, sis, and it just flew right by you."

"So, should I say that 'Chevroness' dumped Ambush to strike out on her own?

Alicia spat air from her lips. "When we're up for a Grammy? You wish. We're just taking a little break. The tour was rough; you ever been to Shenijen? Laws of physics are bass-ackwards crazy there; makes our music sound way different. And that's not the only world like that, you know. By the end of our tour, my migraines were starting to have baby migraines."

"And now you're going to start a club for amateurs?" Kate laughed. "I fail to see how that's going to relax you, but whatever floats your boat, sis. Good luck with that."

Alicia gave an abrupt and infectious start when the powerful green light suddenly appeared in the corner of Kate's eye, and then moved across her field of vision. Kate winced reflexively, and her eyes trailed the beam to a device held by Mukai, who had appeared almost out of nowhere.

"God, Mukai, you almost made me piss my uniform!" Kate exclaimed, and then exhaled in relief. Her biocomp registered the beam as a combination of magnetic waves used in brain scans, and then suggested a mild sedative injection, which she refused. "Wait," she glanced back to the rows of booths, a nearly impossible notion appearing in her mind, and just as soon dismissed. "You can't possibly be finished checking all those booths already."

"I am." Mukai gave a very casual nod, as if such a feat were nothing. She then pointed her device towards Alicia, who flinched slightly as the green light passed over her.

Kate had been about to protest; technology-wise, Gaea was a slightly backwater world, but then her biocomp brought information of the League's new labor exchange program, which Garrett's data said that Mukai was a part of, to mind. And even in her home dimension, she had been damn good at her work.

A shrill chirp came from Mukai's device.

"A match in brainwave/OnBoard algorithms," Mukai explained before Kate could ask. Her friend cast her liquid black-eyed gaze directly towards Alicia. "She is who we are looking for."

"Wh...Who-?" Kate sputtered at the news, which had not quite registered in her mind, but slowly, like a slow data feed from her biocomp, began to clarify in frightening detail. "I mean what the-? You can't be ... Her? No, no, no!"

Her biocomp flashed several accelerated heart rate warnings as she yanked the device from Mukai. Her suit was capable of performing brain scans of its own, but she had to prove that the programming of Mukai's scanner was faulty. There was no way her sister could be their target. From her hand, tendrils of nanofibers slithered into the device's transmitter, which fed the readouts into her field of vision. The uniform adapted to the device's programming and then released a diode which protruded from her shoulder and scanned Alicia, who stood like a deer frozen in headlights. As it had on the device, it came back positive.

Suddenly cold all over, Kate backed away from her sister, her steps halting and trembling as Mukai placidly watched on. How the hell could her own sister be MAGI? This seemed a nightmare of multiple levels of wrongness. Her voice was a pained groan when she finally spoke. "No. God, Aly … why?"

Her expression as immutable as Mukai's, Alicia stepped forward. She opened her mouth to speak, but whether it was to deny or explain, Kate never knew, as several things happened at once.

The air grew colder, and Kate knew that it was not because of her emotional state, especially when a buzz and priority message from her biocomp issued the alarm.

WARNING. MULTIPLE SUBSPACE RIFTS DETECTED.

Kate tensed inwardly, but loosened her body to a combat-ready stance. She felt the weapons forming in her uniform's mass reservoirs, but refrained from ejecting them.

How many? She sent the thought to her biocomp.

NINE RIFTS TOTAL. LEAGUE I.F.F. SIGNAL CONFIRMED IN FIVE: FOUR, FIVE, SIX, SEVEN, AND EIGHT O'CLOCK FROM CURRENT POSITION. SIGNAL NEGATIVE AT ELEVEN, TWELVE, TWELVE-THIRTY, AND ONE O'CLOCK FROM CURRENT POSITION.

The air – no, it was space itself – rippled from behind and in front of her, and behind where Alicia stood. From the rifts in back, a small force of C-class enforcers appeared, armed with magnetic rail rifles, and shielded with thick spidersilk vests and black helmets. A clear spark of consternation flashed through Kate in the midst of her conflicting emotions. Having backup unrequested, and with this much overkill in weaponry, showed a complete lack of faith on the director's part. Garrett well knew that an A-class was more than capable of bringing in one girl, her sister or not.

But then, the beings who stepped out of the rifts behind Alicia snuck doubt into her confidence. Their silver cloaks confused her for a moment, but as their forms clarified once they emerged from the event horizon, they were quite different: off-planers all, each from a different dimension. One was female, green-skinned, and with hair that looked like electrical wiring. Another was ethereal and fairy-like, with wings that folded over her willowy features, honey blonde hair, and cloak, like sparkling veins running through its diaphanous material. Another was wide-bodied and brutish, like a werewolf and gorilla mixed together, while another had a face so heavily tattooed, it was impossible to determine anything at all about him.

"Hey now... no need to get hostile, sis," Alicia said, making a gentle placating gesture —one the enforcers responded to with the harmonized crescendo of their weapons' accelerators powering up.

"Stand down!" Kate ordered, giving a stern gesture to the enforcers. But they held their positions. Kate gaped, half in irritation, half in fear.

"They won't listen to you," the green-skinned one said in an unexpectedly high voice. "Their orders come from the director himself."

"W- what do you want?" Kate demanded, the fingers on her gloved hand extending into claws, and retracting in response to her confusion. She pointed at Alicia and the assembled MAGI. Were they MAGI? There was no way to know, but her gut instinct practically screamed an affirmative. "You've never appeared anywhere en masse."

"Haven't we?" Green Skin said, almost amused.

"What's going on, then?" Kate demanded. "Why is my sister one of you?"

"This isn't what you think," Alicia said in a calm, but stern voice. "In fact, nothing you see here is."

"Not your job, not the League... Your whole life after Cybersoft has been practically a lie," Green Skin said.

"How do you know about Cybersoft?" Kate said, ignoring the foolishness of that question. It didn't take a hacker to find out her job history, after all. "Aly, please! Why are you with them?"

"I've always been with them," Alicia replied matter-of-factly. "Katie, there's so much we want to tell you, but ... now's not the time, you know? And they know too much already."

"'They'? Who are 'they'?" Alicia said, and swallowed hard against a dry throat.

"The League," Green Skin replied.

"We can tell you more later," Alicia said.

"Enough talk," Mukai said, boldly stepping towards Alicia, as if the assembled MAGI were invisible to her. She reached into the obi sash of her uniform and removed a pistol.

"Mukai, what the hell are you doing?" Kate said through gritted teeth. Her biocomp made a series of shrill medical warnings which she effectively silenced with a thought.

"She must be arrested, or terminated," Mukai said.

"Are you out of your freaking mind?" Kate exclaimed. "That's my sister; there's no way in hell you're going to kill her!"

"We have our orders, friend Kate."

"No. My orders," Kate said with finality. "With all due respect, Mukai, you're not an enforcer; you're a ..." she paused as her translation matrix sought the correct word in Glossiu, "... a 'techie'." She shifted her gaze back to her sister. "Aly. Come with me to League HQ; we can talk about this. If worse comes to worst, my lawyers can defend -"

Mukai's gunshot echoed in the restaurant, and in Kate's mind, it became the only sound, fragmented by the image of horror that broke her: Alicia's lifeless body falling to the ground, a ribbon of blood from her wounded skull, the only image in her mind's eye.

She did not know who screamed: herself, Mukai, the enforcers, the MAGI, or even the customers as they fled in panicked terror, but in the corner of her mind that could analyze, she knew the machine had taken over. In the end, when the blood and various off-plane ichors painted the still-repairing stage and floor, and the molecule-thin blades retracted into her uniform, Kate knew that the present scream belonged to her. Exploding grief and anguish and guilt echoed into a crescendo of pain...

...And then vanished.

The world was then replaced with the oddest – and most unpleasant – mix of sensations: a combination of severe vertigo and planar dysphoria: the result of shifting dimensions too rapidly. She retched into a prepared bucket, as a voice spoke soothing words to her. She felt something like a hand upon her back, holding her thick black hair away from her face as the contents of her stomach emptied in the backwash from the horrifying shock to her senses.

"There, there," the voice said. Through her sickness, Kate realized by tone and accent that it was Dr. Galt who spoke to her, and that it was one of his pseudopods upon her back instead of his tiny, ugly hands. "The sickness is commonplace for what you went through. You passed, you know."

"Passed..?" Kate quavered in the midst of coughing after the nausea passed. She spat out the acidic remnants of bile and gingerly wiped her mouth with the back of her hand. A glass of water was presented to her, and she accepted it, taking small sips as to not set off the nausea again. "W ... what happened? Where's Aly? Mukai? I was at Pink's ... I think. I saw the MAGI ..."

"You were sedated, and hooked to a VRSense network," the doctor said, letting go of Kate's hair as she struggled to sit up in the chair. "The mission, the betrayal: all of it was a simulation. All part of your psych exam."

The totality of everything that had happened, and the scope of the doctor's words at last registered. But strangely, she made little reaction to it. Her body still seemed to not accept it.

"So none of it happened?" Kate swallowed another sip of water that had suddenly gone tepid in her mouth. How'd you sedate...?" She froze with cold realization. "The tea!"

"I ... ah ... apologize for the deception, Lieutenant Barnes." His tone was shaky and mawkish and he began to stutter. It became clear to Kate that the Doctor was beginning to feel the full brunt of her emotions. "B-but we had to give you a s-s-simulation that you would accept ... as completely real."

"You didn't have to do it the last time," Kate's voice came out distant and hollow as her initial shock receded and slowly gave way to burning rage. This was nothing else but a violation. The little four-armed creature had put her under and stuck her brain in a computer, running it through scenarios like a rat in a maze. Screw the purpose; this was akin to rape.

"W-we have t-to randomize the test for each p-p-participant, so that the r-results cannot be manip- manipulated by familiarity," the doctor attempted to explain in a voice that cracked like a squeaky wagon wheel. But by now, Kate was beyond either listening or caring. Her eyes downcast, she forced back the tirade that was building in her throat. "And you have to appreciate t-the ultimate harmlessness of ... of the whole ordeal."

Something inside Kate snapped.

"Harmless?" She shot out of the seat, and in one fluid bionic movement, slid forward and grabbed the doctor by the collar of his bodysuit. She glared death into the beady green eyes that were set into the doctor's profusely sweating face. Baring her teeth as her biocomp rippled with weapons options and warnings, she noticed in her peripheral vision the dark patch that had begun to grow in the lower part of the doctor's uniform, as well as a sudden acrid acetone stench that grew in the air.

"You made me watch while one of my best friends killed my sister, you misshapen little kridball!" She stepped forward, and the doctor staggered backwards, his sweat exuding the pungent smell of acetone ever more. "Well, if you think that was harmless, then maybe you'll think this –" She narrowed the width of the heel on her foot padding, and stomped hard on a supporting pseudopod, "– is harmless!"

The doctor howled in pain. A black ichor from his wounded appendage stained the carpet as he collapsed against the wall behind him, exploding a string of expletives in his guttural native tongue. The biocomp offered a translation, and Kate declined as she stormed out of the lab. Several league techies gave her a wide berth when the exit door slid open.

The full force of her emotions came out much later, after the tedium of the calibration tests, when Kate at long last removed the uniform. It hurt like hell as it peeled off of her body in the shower stall, breaking some of her skin. Tiny rivulets of blood washed down the drain as she collapsed to the floor and huddled into a ball, her legs drawn against herself under the warm water's constant assault upon her raw skin. Truly alone now, away from the prying eyes of cameras and her uniform's biocomp, she cried.

Kate's true shame burned like a wound much deeper within. If it were weakness the doctor had been searching for, then he had indeed found it. Through all the implants and the near-invulnerable protection the uniform offered, an enforcer, the League's most elite defense force, was still a frail being in mind. Perhaps this was the reason that not a tear that Kate shed was from the pain that the nanomaterial had left behind.

THE END

The GRID Traveler series

If you like fast-paced space fight scenes, story arcs told episodically with nods to the great Space Opera writers, wonderful character development, then you'll love J Carrell Jones' fascinating world where ancient alien nano-technology is the force behind Magick, and the good guys really are good.

After searching the galaxy for centuries, The Most High Goddess found planet Necron, the origin of Magick. They also discovered Captain Sean Blakemore is one of a handful of humans with the ancient alien DNA that can unlock the planet's vast powers.

Sean Blakemore, Commander of the GRID Battlecruiser Reginald L Johnson, wallowed in self-loathing. He drank too much, suffered from depression, and swam in self-pity. He figured life could not suck any worse when he received new orders. He had to hand the Johnson over to another commanding officer. God hated him he thought.

Then . . . Dr. Loggar, head scientist in charge of this new mission, drew him into the semi-secret world of The Most High Goddess. She gave him hope.

The GRID Traveler series is a story of Sean's redemption, from rock bottom to discovering Humankind's true origins and possibly its inevitable future.

Cassini Finds Global Ocean in Saturn's Moon Enceladus

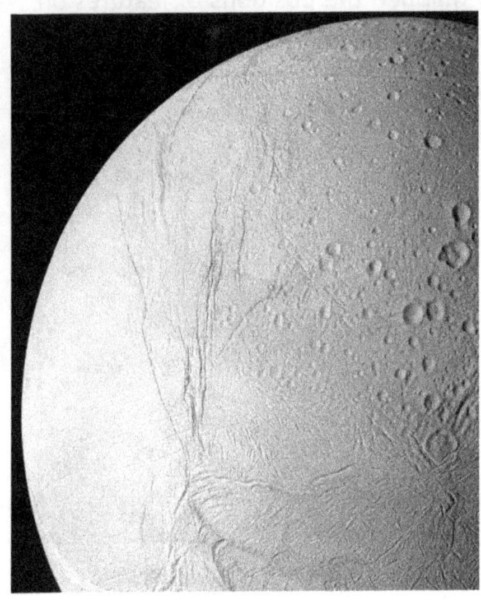

A global ocean lies beneath the icy crust of Saturn's geologically active moon Enceladus, according to new research using data from NASA's Cassini mission.

Researchers found the magnitude of the moon's very slight wobble, as it orbits Saturn, can only be accounted for if its outer ice shell is not frozen solid to its interior, meaning a global ocean must be present.

The finding implies the fine spray of water vapor, icy particles and simple organic molecules Cassini has observed coming from fractures near the moon's south pole is being fed by this vast liquid water reservoir. The research is presented in a paper published online this week in the journal Icarus.

Previous analysis of Cassini data suggested the presence of a lens-shaped body of water, or sea, underlying the moon's south polar region. However, gravity data collected during the spacecraft's several close passes over the south polar region lent support to the possibility the sea might be global. The new results -- derived using an independent line of evidence based on Cassini's images -- confirm this to be the case.

"This was a hard problem that required years of observations, and calculations involving a diverse collection of disciplines, but we are confident we finally got it right," said Peter Thomas, a Cassini imaging team member at Cornell University, Ithaca, New York, and lead author of the paper.

Cassini scientists analyzed more than seven years' worth of images of Enceladus taken by the spacecraft, which has been orbiting Saturn since mid-2004. They carefully mapped the positions of features on Enceladus -- mostly craters -- across hundreds of images, in order to

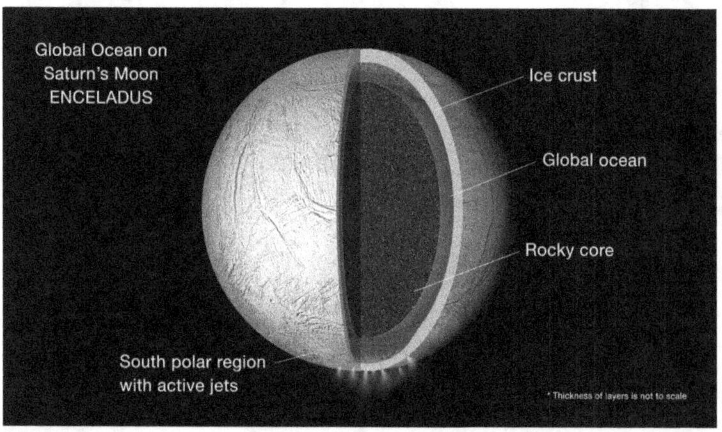

measure changes in the moon's rotation with extreme precision.

As a result, they found Enceladus has a tiny, but measurable wobble as it orbits Saturn. Because the icy moon is not perfectly spherical -- and because it goes slightly faster and slower during different portions of its orbit around Saturn -- the giant planet subtly rocks Enceladus back and forth as it rotates.

The team plugged their measurement of the wobble, called a libration, into different models for how Enceladus might be arranged on the inside, including ones in which the moon was frozen from surface to core.

"If the surface and core were rigidly connected, the core would provide so much dead weight the wobble would be far smaller than we observe it to be," said Matthew Tiscareno, a Cassini participating scientist at the SETI Institute, Mountain View, California, and a co-author of the paper. "This proves that there must be a global layer of liquid separating the surface from the core."

The mechanisms that might have prevented Enceladus' ocean from freezing remain a mystery. Thomas and colleagues suggest a few ideas for future study that might help resolve the question, including the surprising possibility that tidal forces due to Saturn's gravity could be generating much more heat within Enceladus than previously thought.

"This is a major step beyond what we understood about this moon before, and it demonstrates the kind of deep-dive discoveries we can make with long-lived orbiter missions to other planets," said co-author Carolyn Porco, Cassini imaging team lead at Space Science Institute, Boulder, Colorado, and visiting scholar at the University of California, Berkeley. "Cassini has been exemplary in this regard."

The unfolding story of Enceladus has been one of the great triumphs of Cassini's long mission at Saturn. Scientists first detected signs of the moon's icy plume in early 2005, and followed up with a series of discoveries about the material gushing from warm fractures near its south pole. They announced strong evidence for a regional sea in 2014, and more recently, in 2015, they shared results that suggest hydrothermal activity is taking place on the ocean floor.

Cassini is scheduled to make a close flyby of Enceladus on Oct. 28, in the mission's deepest-ever dive through the moon's active plume of icy material. The spacecraft will pass a mere 30 miles (49 kilometers) above the moon's surface.

The Cassini-Huygens mission is a cooperative project of NASA, ESA (European Space Agency) and the Italian Space Agency. NASA's Jet Propulsion Laboratory in Pasadena, California, manages the mission for the agency's Science Mission Directorate in Washington. JPL is a division of the California Institute of Technology in Pasadena. The Cassini imaging operations center is based at SSI. The California Institute of Technology in Pasadena manages JPL for NASA.

For more information about Cassini, visit:

http://www.nasa.gov/cassini

http://saturn.jpl.nasa.gov

Media Contact

Preston Dyches
Jet Propulsion Laboratory, Pasadena, Calif.
818-354-7013
preston.dyches@jpl.nasa.gov

Dwayne Brown / Laurie Cantillo
NASA Headquarters, Washington
202-358-1726 / 202-358-1077
dwayne.c.brown@nasa.gov / laura.l.cantillo@nasa.gov

2015-298

AFRO-MAN
AND THE PROTECTORS OF THE BOOK OF KNOWLEDGE
FUN FOR THE ENTIRE FAMILY!
KNOWLEDGE IS POWER!
AFRO-MAN
THE ANIMATED SERIES
EPISODE #2
DVD
AFRO-MAN
& THE PROTECTORS OF THE BOOK OF KNOWLEDGE
THE ANIMATED SERIES
AFRO-MAN
BUY NOW!
THE ANIMATED SERIES
WWW.AFROMANKIDSSPACE.COM

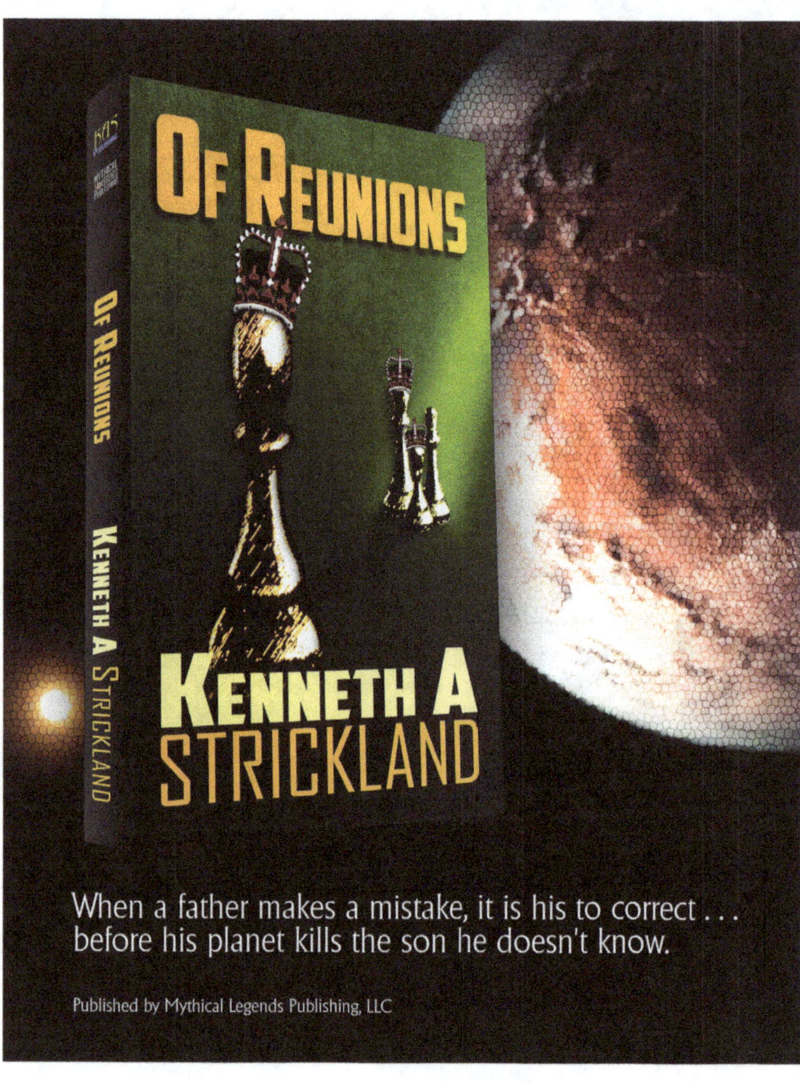

When a father makes a mistake, it is his to correct . . . before his planet kills the son he doesn't know.

Published by Mythical Legends Publishing, LLC

**This is a KAS Publishing
and
Mythical Legends Publishing venture**

Of Reunions

Kenneth A. Strickland

Sci-Fantasy
eBook and Paperback

Michael John Stone hadn't known his mother fell in love with a man from another world.
Then, one day, the man disappeared and life moved forward.
Decades later, the man, and his planet, needed Michael.

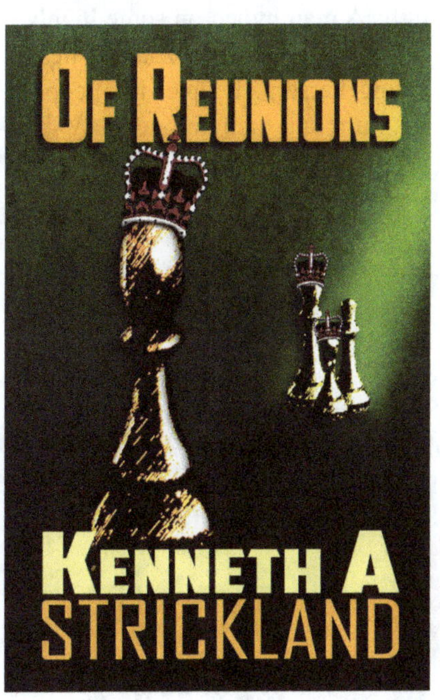

On a world where his very existence was illegal, Michael discovered what he truly valued. His father discovered the depths of self-delusion and both struggled against powerful enemies to reveal the rings that bind together their souls - the soulmage within.

RAGE

J Carrell Jones

Karen Bechard, UN Agent, thought the flight from the US to Europe was going to be routine. It was in mid flight where everything turned ugly. A man hyped on some highly addictive drug goes zombie flesh eating berserk. People die, people get hurt, and then no one to fly the plane. What is an agent to do? And, that was the easy part of the day, of which was turning out to be a Four Horsemen trampling humanity scenario and Karen had to be on her A-game.

If you like fast-paced heroic action dished out by a badass female agent then this book is for you. Bond, Salt? Step aside. This new girl is taking names and kicking

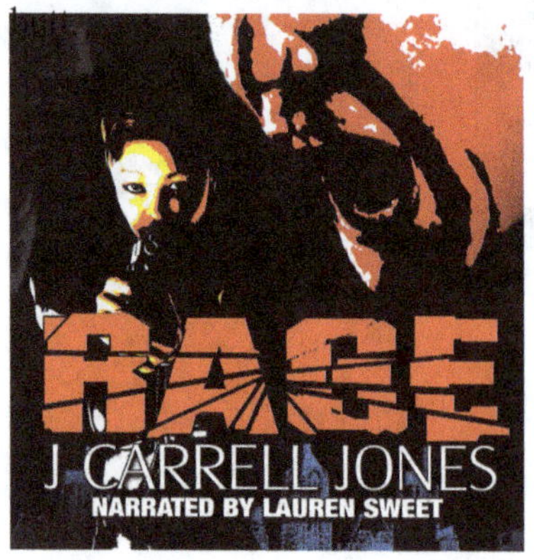

Enemy Me

J Carrell Jones

Sci-Fi Thriller
eBook, Paperback, and Audiobook

Pete Walker died . . . again . . . and again . . . and again . . .
The very profitable pharmaceutical behemoth Forever Life, Inc. was ready to start Human trials using a new wonder drug that was going to liberate the world. Every disease known - cured. Every handicap or birth defect - eliminated. You don't like your hair texture? Your eye color? Skin color? Height? One small pill taken at night, a short drug induced coma, and several days later - a new you. The problem was that Pete feared this new pill would lead to the extinction of humankind. He had to stop Forever Life at any cost. Any. Cost. Which, included his life . . . again . . .

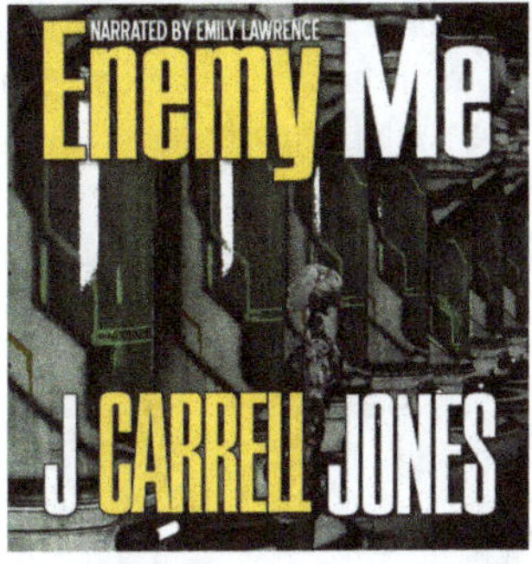

GRID Traveler: Magick Journey

A strategizing adventure board game based off the GRID Traveler book series.

In the GRID Traveler Universe, Magick is possible because of Advanced Ancient Alien Nano Technology (A3NT). Centuries ago, a semi-secret religious organization, known as The Most High Goddess, integrated itself in all aspects of human society. Their goal was to discover the origin of Magick and once humans ventured out into space they eventually did find the origin.

In our distant history, Aliens visited earth. The Aliens performed what humans perceived as magick, which created our belief in magick and the rise of The Most High Goddess. Magick Journey begins about a hundred years into the future at the end of the GRID Traveler Trilogy series. The board game is an alternate history in which some of the main characters of the book have become powerful Necronians that visit the "present" timeline of the main game characters. Some characters are portraited as regular players AND Necronians.

The Game Crafters

YouTube Video Review

Double-Cross My Heart
Brandon Hill

Sci-Fantasy
Paranormal Romance
Thriller
Paperback and Hardback

Turned at a tender age, and left with no memory of her human life, Elisa, the beloved adopted daughter of Talante, has had many obvious difficulties in her near two centuries of life, but none so frustrating as her inability to find love - that is until a dire mission leads her to Derek, another vampire turned in his formative years, and the de facto leader of a clan of vagabonds: vampires who choose to take no sides in the ten millennia long war between her symbiotic clan and the dominating breed of her father's hated enemy. But her happiness is only a prelude to heartbreak as she learns secrets of a past she thought erased, which may cost her the trust and love of the one who holds the greatest portion of her heart.

Beneath CatsEye
Patricia I. Williams

Sci-Fantasy
eBook and Paperback

In the not too distant future, the Earth's corporate giants and surviving governments decide the cleansing of the overpopulated planet is a necessity. In collusion advertising campaigns draw in the desperate, the fanatic and the soldier for the first colonization of an extraterrestrial body. The ships were quickly filled with volunteers, willing . . . or not.

At the end of a long journey, the few military leaders observed the disaster that spun below them. Cold, bombarded and fading, their new home was clearly less than advertised. So the scientist went to work, to speed up the process toward occupying the planet. Years later as the ships' occupants disembarked, hungry eyes looked on.

Four Corners

Kenneth A. Strickland

Sci-Fantasy
Alternate History
Paperback

In 1945, the town of Four Corners, Georgia found they were having babies born with four-arms. It happened on the black side of town first, and they tried to keep it a secret . . . until the first white babies were born with four-arms. Now the two sides of the town had to come together to save itself and regain its balance. This story has heart, humor, and action as the town copes when the discovery begins with one of its own after a big rig truck crash.

Four Corners is never going to be the same . . . again . . .

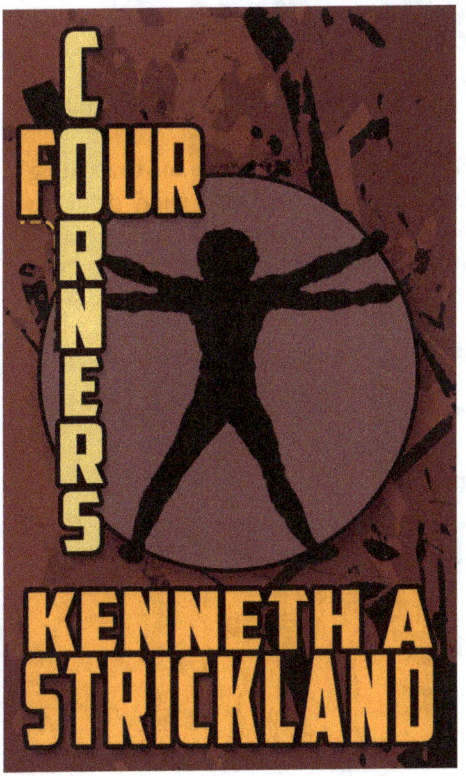

https://www.thegamecrafter.com/games/inappropriate

Inappropriate

A fast-paced fun filled salacious card game for consenting mature adults.

This is a fast-paced fun filled salacious card game for consenting mature adults.It is one part strip poker, one part party drinking game, one part calculating game. The winner is the only player with some clothes left on or the last player holding at least one card.

Players can agree to make "Inappropriate" strictly a drinking card game, an only last player standing game, a strip poker game, or all of the above.

Available at **The Game Crafters**
$23.99 Retail
2 - 6 players

Average 30 minutes or less per set
Party card game
Adults Only

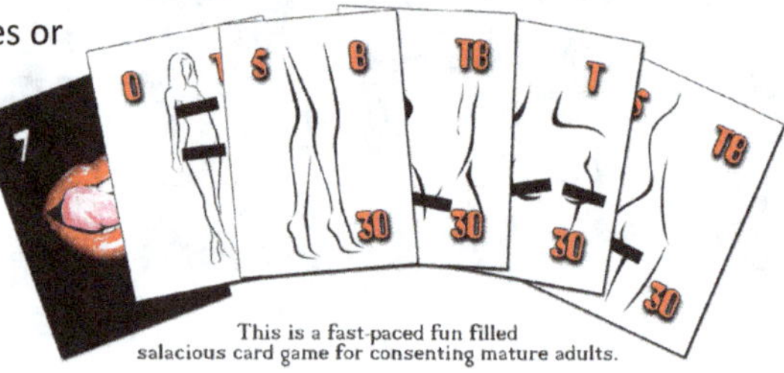

This is a fast-paced fun filled salacious card game for consenting mature adults.